FROM THE EDGE OF

DARKNESS

FROM THE EDGE OF

DARKNESS

By MILES KENT

"I am enough of an artist to draw freely upon my imagination. Imagination is more important than knowledge. Knowledge is limited. Imagination encircles the world."

Albert Einstein

To my wonderful wife Niki. Without you none of this is possible.

1

Space, vast and empty, has been a source of fascination for humans throughout time. Over the centuries, some of the greatest human minds have been dedicated to better understanding our place in the universe, with technology increasing our ability to see further and further from our home planet. It is hard to imagine not knowing what the outer planets look like in granular detail, but it wasn't until the Pioneer 10 spacecraft was launched towards the largest of the outer planets that we caught our first glimpse of the gas giant Jupiter in detail. But that wasn't enough to quench the thirst for knowledge even further away from Earth and humans continued to develop more technology to see even further out.

Every 176 years, the outer planets align with Earth. The last time this happened was in the 1970s when the planets strung out like a loosely fitted pearl necklace across space with Earth, the two gas giants Jupiter & Saturn, followed by the ice giants Uranus and Neptune. Humans were still in the very early stages of space flight when NASA scientists sat down in the mid-1960s and calculated that this rare alignment may give them the unique opportunity to explore the outer planets.

The Space Race was well and truly on with the Soviets having sent Yuri Gagarin into space to complete one orbit of our planet in April 1961. The United States was planning the next big move with the Apollo missions already underway with extra impetuous added following the first manned space flight. The USA was wounded, needed to come back and had both the political will and the financial power to do so. Landing the first man on the moon dominated American thinking and it was imperative they landed there before the Soviets and set themselves a target of 1970 at the very latest.

Whilst landing on the moon took up most of the United States' bandwidth, the extra funding that resulted enabled them to look beyond just that. NASA was created in the late 1950s and several departments had been moved across to the new civilian space agency. The Jet Propulsion Laboratory (JPL) was moved over in exactly that way when, in 1958, it was transferred from the jurisdiction of the Army to that of NASA. It is a federally funded research and development centre which is managed by the California Institute of Technology (Caltech).

Through the 1960's the JPL worked on and sent robotic probes to the moon, with the Ranger spacecraft, then progressed to moon landings with the Surveyor project. JPL specialised in robotic probes and it didn't take long for them to draw up proposals to send probes to the outer planets using the gravity of each planet in the rare alignment to power the probes between giant entities. Eventually, the two Voyager spacecraft were designed and built to investigate the far reaches of our solar system and measure and investigate the outer planets.

The two Voyager spacecraft are identical. They weigh 773kg each and comprise several scientific instruments, two cameras and an antenna that looks like a 1980s TV satellite receiver. Both spacecraft have a golden phonograph record which contains both sounds and images depicting life on Earth and the human race. Power is supplied by three radioisotope thermoelectric generators. They are powered by plutonium-238 and provided approximately 470 W at

30 volts DC when launched. The mission was too far from the Sun to use solar power and the radioactive material was found to be perfect to generate enough heat to be converted into electricity.

Voyager 2 was the first of the two spacecraft to be launched and was sent towards the outer planets on the 20th of August 1977, flying on a Titan-Centaur expendable rocket. It hurtled towards the outer planets and was followed less than a month later by its twin. Whilst launched second, Voyager 1 was on a more direct route so was expected to reach Jupiter first.

Voyager 1 was launched on 5th September 1977 from Florida. Both spacecraft were expected to reach the outer planets and their expected life was around five years. Deep into the 21st century, both craft are now in interstellar space, still communicating with Earth, still helping man understand what is beyond the pull of our own star. Whilst some systems are now redundant, they continue to fly and we can but wonder what they can see. On February 14th 1990, Voyager 1 took its last photograph, The pale blue dot showed just how tiny the earth appears from the outer reaches of the solar system. Sadly, the cameras on both spacecraft are now one of the many redundant systems, never to be used again.

There are many theories as to what exists in interstellar space and beyond. Some believe that the sheer number of planets already discovered means that, purely on the balance of probabilities, something else must exist out there. Some scientists also theorise that life outside Earth does not exist. Professor Stephen Hawking was not one of them and went a step further than others. He was convinced there is intelligent life beyond what can be found on earth. As humans sent more and more messages out to space, he warned that any civilisation that could actually read a message would likely need to be billions of years ahead of us in development and he went even further, commenting "If so they will be vastly more powerful and may not see us as any more valuable than we see bacteria." Hawking went as far as to compare alien life coming to Earth to the fate of native people when Columbus discovered the Americas.

So the warnings are there, from a remarkable human being with an understanding far beyond most of us. Yet despite this stark warning, we continue to reach out beyond our own planet into space, vast and empty........or so we thought.

2

Monday 5th September 1977, Pasadena, California: "My dear fellow, how I would love to be in your place, not a care in the world." Larry Manning was walking with his faithful best friend, Charlie, a three-year-old Golden Retriever. Charlie had a fascination with everything, every blade of grass, every stone, every tree. "Come on old boy, the rocket will take off without me at this rate, imagine that!" He smiled to himself as he looked down. Charlie could stretch a ten-minute walk out for an hour as he flipped each item over, sniffed it, and then moved on to the next. On this morning that promised to be so very hectic, however, Larry was enjoying taking his time looking up to the sky as they ambled along. Larry lived in a one-story white-painted wooden house on a road opposite a small wooded park. The park was very neat and had a path through the middle and street lights across its length with the path snaking around the park to the entrances at either end. The park was popular with locals and their dogs and every few hundred feet was a park bench which was often used by locals to eat and read their books.

They passed other dog walkers as they travelled through the park, with Charlie barely acknowledging their existence as he continued his thorough investigation of everything he came across. Larry looked at him and smiled. 'The life of a dog!' he said quietly. 'So simple and so happy'. He reflected on Charlie's attitude to every day, treating it as a brand new adventure. 'Carpe diem, Charlie', he whispered to his faithful friend as they continued along the path.

It was a gentle early fall morning and the remnants of late summer were still in the air, the stifling heat which would inevitably scorch the rest of the day was still a few hours away. It was like summer but it wasn't, you could smell the change in the air as the dry months gave way to a slightly gentler Californian season, with the leaves starting to change colour and Californians starting to prepare themselves for the colder months ahead. Of course, being California it wasn't cold, certainly not compared to further north in the country, but Larry was strangely sensitive to changes in temperature and had decided to venture out in his coat and scarf covering up his work clothes for the first time that year.

As they walked together, one of Larry's neighbours walked past with what looked like a breakfast roll in her hand. He acknowledged her with a reciprocated smile and nod as they passed each other. He took a deep breath in through his nose and could almost taste the warm sausage patty with freshly fried egg together with something sweeter, 'probably ketchup' he thought. "Well Charlie," he said, "I think that's a sign that it's time for something to eat. Mom has made something special this morning buddy". Charlie gazed up and engaged Larry with his deep brown eyes, jowls slightly moist from the morning dew and an auburn leaf sticking out from his bottom front teeth and covering his nose. Larry wondered if Charlie knew the leaf was there and smiled.

As they exited the park, crossed the road and went through the gate, Larry could see his wife in the kitchen making breakfast for the two of them. The windows were moist with condensation, on the inside he presumed, down in no small part to the fact his wife didn't like to cook with the windows open. "The fragrance of my cooking is a gift for us to enjoy, not our neighbours" she would often say in response to Larry's complaints about soggy windows. Even with the view through the window somewhat limited, Larry could see she was happy and appeared to be singing to herself, or possibly the radio, as she moved gracefully around the kitchen like a ballerina. Tall and slim with short, dark, wavy hair she was as beautiful now as the day he had met her 25 years previously.

Larry was particularly reflective this morning as the first phase of his life's work neared its conclusion. As he opened the door, he was immediately assaulted by a delicious blend of culinary aroma, Charlie charged through the house and could be heard lapping water enthusiastically from his bowl in the laundry room. "How was the daily drag dear?" called Larry's wife, Barbara. "It surprises me how he actually manages to work up a thirst" she chuckled as she poured Larry's coffee. Taking Charlie for his walk wasn't one of Larry's favourite tasks but this morning it was different. He took his packet of Lucky Strikes from the top left breast pocket of his shirt and pulled the red tag, separating the cellophane wrapping. Larry had fought in the Korean War in the 1950s and Lucky Strike was included in the American ration packs. He'd smoked them ever since. He took a cigarette out of the pack, placed it gently between his lips, sparked his zippo lighter into life and lit his cigarette. He enthusiastically took the first draw, like a child trying to suck ice cream through a straw as the end glowed gently and lines of smoke crept up into the air to give the smells of food more than a hint of tobacco. As the light smell of petrol from the zippo lighter still lingered in the air, Larry wandered into the kitchen and picked up his coffee.

"Thanks Bar," said Larry as he smelled the freshly made mug of strong black coffee.

"Over easy?" she asked, as she shuffled the frying pan back and forth. She didn't cook breakfast every morning, she was too busy herself as a writer for the local newspaper and was constantly on the hunt for the next big story. But this was a big day for Larry and she intended to treat him like a king.

"Yes please dear" he responded as he took a second, less intense puff of his cigarette. Charlie trotted into the kitchen with his jowls dripping with water having finished splashing it around the laundry room in a vain attempt to rehydrate himself, walked over to his soft dark blue bed in the corner and made himself comfortable. Making himself comfortable typically involved ten laps of the tiny bed and a contented sigh to indicate he was happy with his lot and today was no different.

"When do you think you'll be home tonight honey? I don't mind but I'd like to make us something nice, or maybe we could go out?" asked Barbara as she filled the washing-up bowl with piping hot water.

"I don't know Bar, it depends on how well things go, there's a lot that could go wrong."

Larry was usually a confident character, however this was truly an ambitious project and, although this phase was now coming to an end, he didn't want to count his chickens. "Maybe hold off for now and do something nice at the weekend?" he continued. Barbara smiled and nodded. She had already eaten her breakfast and was focused on cleaning up so she could get back on top of her own work and Charlie was busy snoring on his bed, dreaming of being given a bone the size of a rocket, no doubt.

Larry finished his breakfast, hugged Barbara and petted Charlie as he went through the front door. After his morning fix of caffeine, he was now ready to take on the rigours of the day and he walked with a bounce, his feet crunching onto the gravel footpath.

"Wait!" Barbara called after him. "You've forgotten your lunch!" Larry smiled as he turned back to see Barbara, standing in the doorway with her pinny still on, waving his metal lunchbox around. He took the lunchbox, got into his brown 1965 Chevrolet Impala, started the engine, drove out of the driveway and turned left towards work.

It was a short twenty-minute drive to the office but that gave him ample time to focus on the day ahead and the momentous nature of it. As the light darted between the trees and pierced through the glass of his windshield, Larry started to think through the timings of the day's events and double-check that everything was ready. As the Jet

Propulsion Laboratory swung into view, Larry felt his top right breast pocket, located his pass card, took it out and held it outside of his car window as he drove past security. "Big day today Larry? Good luck," called Bob the security guard as the car passed by.

"Thanks, Bob, hopefully we won't need it".

He pulled to the left of the large, square, box-shaped, glass-fronted main building and aimed for the access gate. Today, he took particular notice of the large blue NASA sign towards the top right of the building and was brimming with pride as he showed his pass at the second guard post and was waved through. Larry had always parked his car in the same place and out of habit did so again that morning, pulling on his parking break like he was lifting weights. He opened the rear driver's door and took his lunch box, flask and leather briefcase, put the briefcase over his left shoulder and closed the door with his knee. It was a secure car park so he didn't bother to lock the car.

As he walked towards the building he could hear the California wildlife performing a chorus in the background and it felt like a welcome. He swiped his card to gain access to the building and made his way up the cold, concrete stairs, to the fifth floor. A very sterile building, it could take some time to learn where the various offices and labs were around the complex but Larry had been there most of his adult working life and knew it like the back of his hand. As he walked into the main project office on the fifth floor he was pleased with the energy and buzz that greeted him. A sizeable office, it was officially called the Voyager control centre but was known simply as 'the office' by all who worked there. Capable of housing fifty people comfortably it was arranged in pods based on functionality with computers on each desk with multiple screens, surrounded by a blue plastic housing and each fitted with a white phone. Above each POD hung a small white sign from the ceiling with the name of the department and every few feet a small TV screen was suspended from above. Whilst it was a sizeable room, every inch of space was used and you couldn't walk through the office too quickly for fear of falling over wires and electrical equipment.

Voyager 1 was undergoing final remote checks before the proposed launch later that day. Larry went up to the main podium, put his briefcase under his desk and his lunch and coffee between two of the screens and gazed up over the light fog of cigarette smoke. "Folks, can I have your attention please?" He was a naturally quiet man and when he made loud announcements he would lower his voice as if he were acting which forced people to listen and not just treat him as background noise. The loud hum of people stopped and everybody looked up at Larry. "Ok, nothing has changed from yesterday, let's remember this isn't the first time we've done this." Dr Larry Manning was a 46-year-old with a doctorate in Aeronautics and astronautics from MIT, had worked within the lab for the last 20 years and was brimming with experience. Unusually personable for a man with his level of intellect he was well respected within both the academic world and NASA. Larry was chosen as the team leader for the Voyager Mission which encompassed both spacecraft and this was his first assignment in such a senior position. He was incredibly proud, but also slightly nervous. Slightly unkempt, he wore a pair of dark brown slacks, a beige shirt with a sleeveless cream sweater over the top and his tie peeking out from the bottom. Thick-rimmed glasses decorated his face. Married to the love of his life, they had no children and his life was devoted to his work, his wife and his beloved K-9 best friend.

Voyager 1 was in Florida at the Kennedy Space Centre waiting to be thrust into space later that day. The team had been split between watching Voyager 2's progress and readying Voyager 1. Larry was worried they'd taken their eye off the ball since the Voyager 2 launch and he was in no mood to contemplate failure when he addressed the team. "OK, the weather is looking good for 08:55 hrs our time. The focus has to be total, people, we can't afford to screw this one up despite our previous success, get that out of your mind. Today, we launch Voyager 1 towards a journey of discovery." It crossed his mind that this little speech was for his benefit as much as anybody else's. Larry followed his little talk by reaching into his briefcase where he pulled out an envelope with the presidential seal clear on the outside. 'I have received this message from the President.' There were gasps in the room. Larry continued, "I'll read it in full:

'Dear Dr Manning,

Please accept my best wishes, on behalf of the American People, for the forthcoming launch of the Voyager 1 Spacecraft. With this and the recent launch of Voyager 2, you embody the hopes and dreams of our nation. As we watch the voyager spacecraft break the shackles of Earth's orbit and speed through space, I and the world will be watching, in awe of your strength of spirit. As we begin the adventure to the outer planets know this: your country and your president are behind you,

God speed,

J.Carter'

Larry had a taste for the dramatic, likely born from his love of amateur dramatics, a hobby he enjoyed with Barbara. As the eyes fixed on him as he spoke, the countdown clock on a TV screen above his head continued the countdown to the launch. Amongst those watching was the newest member of the team, Debra Johnson, a 21-year-old doctorate student.

Debra hailed from a small town called Greenville in Maine. Situated in Piscataquis County, it is the gateway to the type of wilderness that is famous in the state of Maine's far north and is situated on the southern shore of Maine's largest lake, Moosehead Lake. Debra's childhood was spent in and around the lake and she went back every opportunity she had. She lived with her two parents and had very few friends, preferring to play on her own as a child and explore on her own as a young adult. Without a sibling, she was the focus of all her parent's attention and that suited her fine. She was such a home bird that she elected to read for her undergraduate degree in astrophysics at Harvard, not because it was one of the best universities in the world, but because it was relatively close to home, less than five hours by car and she would return at every opportunity. Debra was five feet eight inches tall, slim and with very pale skin and long blond hair that she wore brushed back and framed by a light blue hair band. She was wearing a white blouse, long light blue skirt and was smoking her fourth cigarette of the day.

The love of Maine was something Debra shared with Larry, who had a beach house in Rockport where he and Barbara would spend their time strolling through the beautifully historic town with Charlie. That was the only thing they shared though as they were two very different characters. Larry drew energy from his relationship with Barbara, Debra was a loner and had no desire to be around anybody, least of all a partner. Intelligent, inquisitive and intense, Debra had managed to gain a place on the program with relative ease having been recommended by her Harvard Professor.

After his brief announcement, Larry took his seat and started to look through some of the data that had been prepared for him, marking areas of interest with his pencil. The hum returned to the room as the rest of the team prepared for the launch and in Florida, final preparations were being made to the Titan rocket upon which Voyager 1 would ride. As the minutes ticked past, the team began to gather around the largest screen as the launchpad in Florida was going through final preparations. It was Debra's turn to hand out the 'good luck' peanuts, a tradition that started in the 1960s and she walked around the crowd of colleagues, offering out the salty snacks. Clear blue skies and a heat haze were the backdrop for the launch and, as the support trusses finally separated from the rocket, the room quietened…..

"10….9….8….7….6….5….4….3….2….1….and we have ignition, we have lift off….vehicle response is normal, tank pressures are normal."

As the Titan rocket rose smoothly into the Floridian morning sky, the team watched in silence back in California, it proved too much for Larry as he sparked up another Lucky Strike cigarette to break the silence.

"Still smooth, little variance…"

As the seconds ticked away and the various stages of the rocket separated from the main body, it became clear the launch was a success. Larry stood up suddenly, "Well done!" as the rest of the room erupted, jumping and shouting at the top of their voices. Joy mixed with relief as Voyager 1 soared high, through the atmosphere and into space to start its long journey to the outer planets.

Larry arrived home in the late evening just as the light of day had given way to the darkness of another clear Californian night and the evening shift of crickets had sparked into their familiar chorus. Larry drove down the tree-lined street just as the lights flickered on for the night. He pulled into the driveway and glanced across to his home, curtains still open and the lights on, as Barbara ran out to congratulate him. As she ran up to him he lifted her off her feet and kissed her smiling mouth.

"We did it!!" Larry shouted excitedly.

"No, Larry, you did it!!" Barbara responded excitedly.

He grabbed his briefcase, flask and lunchbox from the car and followed Barbara into the house where he was greeted by an even more excited Charlie. As was usual, Charlie thought Larry had deserted him when he went to work that morning and his greeting was as much relief that he hadn't been kidnapped as it was that his best friend had come home. He gave Charlie a big hug and received a sizeable lick in return before going back out to the car to close the gate behind him. As he walked out into the garden he looked up just as a shooting star arced across the clear night sky. 'What will you see up there Voyager? What an amazing adventure you've begun.'

3

Present day, Monday, 05:55 hrs, Jet Propulsion Laboratory, Pasadena, California: "Is it that time already?" Jess stretched her long arms upwards, tilting her head back and stretching her neck at the same time. Gus was yawning himself as he placed his black laptop case on the desk next to her.

The office, as it was called, had changed significantly since the mid-1970s. It was now more like an actual office with the control room having moved into a much larger space. It was still a sizeable room with large flat screens on individual desk pods with adapters for laptops and a row of USB inputs next to each screen. Far less clutter than in the seventies, it was a modern environment with all the newest technology, including several large frameless QLED screens which were dotted around on walls. There was an ability to patch into the large screens from any laptop in the office using the superfast building WiFi. The two largest screens in the office had maps tracking the progress of both Voyager spacecraft with the velocity at the bottom and a list of their facts and figures to the side.

Two other things separated the office of the 2020s and that of its predecessor of the 1970s. The first was smoke, this was now a smoke-free building and the remnants of tobacco and tar had long since been scrubbed from the walls. The second was noise, most of those working there now used earbuds so any little noise the computers emitted was confined to the ears of the operative. The far side of the office was now floor-to-ceiling glass and went out to a balcony where workers were encouraged to take time out from their screens regularly and take in the warm Californian air. The importance of hydration was something the lab also now took seriously and modern silver metal water dispensers were also dotted around the room with white paper cone-shaped cups in tubes attached to the machines. Feeding off the main office were conference rooms with digital conferencing facilities together with meeting rooms of various sizes. A modern working environment fit for the 21st century.

Jessica Wilson was a 21-year-old Californian physicist, fresh from graduating college, she had volunteered to cover all of the overnight shifts. She liked how quiet they were as there was no management around to interrupt her thoughts and academic work. Thoughts were something she had plenty of too, a very active mind and an even more active imagination.

Jess lived in an apartment in Pasadena with an old college friend and spent as much time at work or studying as possible. A keen sportswoman she had a passion for long-distance running and competed for her college at the 5000 meters, that wasn't the only sport she loved though and was able to turn her hand to most disciplines. Working during the night meant she could get her training in beforehand whilst still light and she'd often go for a run in the early morning once she had gotten home, away from the full, harsh glare of the sun later in the day.

This morning, similar to others, she already had her training clothes on and was currently sporting black shiny leggings, a white slim-fit long-sleeved training top and dark pink trainers. Like many before her, she was also studying for her doctorate in Geophysics and Space Physics at UCLA and hoped for a long career at NASA and the JPL. Jess was fascinated by the Voyager program and how, at over 45 years and still going, we could still communicate from and learn so much from these ageing spacecraft. They were only built to last five years and so many discoveries had been made over the decades as a direct result. Whilst a number of its systems no longer functioned, like the cameras for example, they were still transmitting back to Earth from billions of miles away.

The Voyager team had been scaled back substantially over the years with most of the original team having retired or moved on to other work either within the Jet Propulsion Laboratory or elsewhere in NASA. Only one of the original team remained working on the project and she was now the senior research fellow and project manager, Debra Johnson, now in her 60's.

Life hadn't changed a great deal for Debra since 1977, she still lived alone and preferred her own company. She had never found love and was now resigned to never doing so. She still returned to Maine from time to time and owned her parent's old home having inherited it when her mother passed away following her father's death a few years before, she would always visit the lake when she returned and thoroughly enjoyed walking around and looking at the wildlife.

Larry had long since retired and lived in a cabin in the North Californian forest with Barbara. In his nineties now and far slower than in his prime, they still walked as much as they could and would still visit their cottage in Maine with their dachshund, Charlie. Lovers of Retrievers, Larry had mistakenly thought that a smaller dog would be less of a commitment, he was wrong. The latest iteration of Charlie was far more demanding than any of his predecessors and much louder too. Whilst Charlie was only ankle height, nobody had told him that and he spent his time strutting around like he was Rottweiler. Despite this, he was the love of their life though and went everywhere with them. Debra still kept in touch with both of them and would often consult with Larry when she was unsure of something, he was as wise as he'd always been and was her perfect sounding board.

"Well nothing too exciting overnight and readings all look normal, they're still hurtling through interstellar space at a rate of knots!"

Jess said. Gus was his usual underwhelmed self and, having never been a morning kinda guy, was at the most underwhelmed point of his day.

"Well I wouldn't expect anything different" he responded, completely deadpan.

He took his computer out of its bag, opened it and pressed his index fingernail into the tiny lower button on the right of the machine. It sprung to life with the fan inside sounding like it was taking its first breath and scrolled through to the encryption screen where Gus typed the day's randomly generated code he read off his digital key ring.

Gus.....or Dr Gus Thompson, was a 29-year-old with a doctorate in space science from UCL in London and was currently on the JPL Postdoctoral program. He was desperate to move to one of the Mars programs and saw Voyager as being a dusty old program that was only still going through luck and nostalgia. He believed the Voyager program's most exciting moments were either way back in its distant past or so far into the future he would be long gone and the instruments on board would have long since switched off. With an application in to transfer to one of the Mars programs having undertaken some research earlier that year, his attention was most definitely elsewhere. Despite this, he was extremely professional and nobody would have known his interest had faded. Gus lived with his husband, Jason and they had a three-year-old child which took most of their attention. Jason was a real estate agent and did more than his fair share of the parenting due to the demands of Gus's job. Jason didn't mind though as he was keen to bond with their son, being naturally far more sensitive than Gus.

"Sorry Jess, any anomalistic readings I need to know about?" He asked as he remembered himself.

"There was a strange reading on Voyager 1 last night. It appeared to slow its velocity suddenly but when I checked a second time it was back to normal. Must have been an instrument malfunction, the signal is so weak."

"I'll keep an eye on it and ask one of the engineers to double-check it today Jess" responded Gus as he straightened out his pale lemon shirt, tucking them into his dark brown corduroy trousers.

"Thanks, I'm off to bed for a few hours and I'll see you this evening" With that, Jess picked up her car keys, lunch box and walked out of the office to her car.

Whilst both Voyager spacecraft still worked, they were prone to strange readings from time to time. As the distance between Earth and the two spacecraft increases, the effort it takes to communicate with them increases, one day in the future it will not be possible at all. Communication is currently managed using the 'Deep Space Network', a trio of giant antennas across three sites, one in Madrid, one in Canberra Australia and the third deep in the Californian Mojave Desert. It takes a day for any communications to reach the crafts and the same back, any response from them was a couple of days away and by the time those readings had reached Jess, they would already be well out of date. As such, the solution was often to just wait and see if the problem rectified itself, it often did. Should that not happen, an engineer would look at what the issue may be and create a workaround.

Gus put his piping hot coffee on the table, squinted at the large computer screen on his desk and looked around the modern but sparse office. It was just gone 6 am and he was the only one in and within the next few hours more would begin their working day. He had a couple of hours on his own to ease into the day. He took a sip of his decaf latte and sat down to review the data from the previous evening. As he looked through the data his eyes were drawn to 0257 that morning. The data showed Voyager 1 moving at around 38000 mph and Voyager 2 at around 35000 until that point. There was a sudden change though at 0257 hrs and the reading showed Voyager 1 at 100mph, then showed minus figures which meant it was moving towards Earth. At 0300 it's shown moving at 38000 mph again. 'What on earth could have made that happen?' He thought out loud as he sat back in his chair. He quickly concluded it must be an error reading. This wasn't the first strange reading they had received but it was still worth talking it through with an engineer when he saw one later in the day.

The remainder of the day passed by with a little more excitement. Gus bumped into Josh Williams, one of the engineers, in the early afternoon. They were both taking in some fresh air in one of the gardens located near the main cafeteria. They ambled past the chugging sprinklers watering the lush green grass and took in the warm dry heat of the afternoon.

"Well Josh, what do you think?" Quizzed Gus.

"I can think of no way that could happen without destroying the spacecraft. That level of deceleration alone would be too much, I think we can probably write that one off as an anomaly. It may be that the high gain antenna briefly pointed away from Earth and we just got a blank reading?"

Gus nodded as he took a bite out of the Turkey Avocado wrap he'd been promising himself all morning and was about to wash down with an ice-cold green tea.

The high-gain antenna sends the data back to Earth. The spacecraft has to be oriented in such a way as to enable the antenna to send the data. If the spacecraft isn't oriented correctly nothing comes back.

"I can check the orientation of the craft but, as you know, it'll take a couple of days before we get a response." Continued Josh. At this stage in Voyager's mission, the team are used to both the time lag and anomalistic readings.

"Thanks" responded Gus as he wiped the remnants of fresh avocado from the side of his mouth, and with that, he walked over to a nearby bench and table to finish his lunch. As often happened, his mind started to wander, consumed by the 'what if' questions. What if they could switch the cameras back on and have a look at what interstellar space looks like, what if this wasn't an anomaly? Gus often thought about what the two Voyager spacecraft could see but that ship had long since sailed, 'even if they had the energy they're probably frozen now' he concluded.

18:00 hrs the same day - Jess walked into the office again looking refreshed and ready for the night ahead. "It feels like I just left. How we doing Gus?" She slapped the lintel above the door as she walked in, an old superstition that most would associate with going into an aircraft. She was wearing blue 501s and a red light-weight woollen sweater. She had gone for a five-mile run before going to bed that morning and, having spent only five hours asleep, had met a friend for coffee in the afternoon. It had been a very sunny day and she felt refreshed as she drove to the lab in the warm early evening sun. She hadn't bothered to take her computer home and had left it under the desk when she left that morning so she reached down, took it out of the case and plugged it in. As she booted it up and the Jet Propulsion Laboratory and NASA logos lit up the screen, she smiled as she reflected on how lucky she was to have her job. Still feeling a little guilty about his shortness that morning, Gus had made Jess a coffee before she arrived and it was on her desk, waiting for her as she booted up her computer.

"Yeah good, oh hey, I asked Josh to check out those readings from last night. He agrees it's probably a mistake but he's running some checks, should get the results in a couple of days."

Having updated Jess, Gus stood up, put his soft herringbone sports jacket on and left. Jess was left alone in the office once more, staring at a screen, drinking strong coffee and reading books. From time to time she broke up the monotony of the night by walking out to the balcony and watching some of the wildlife that could be seen from beyond the window. She often wondered how much about the world the animals know beyond what's in front of their nose. 'That must be nice' she often reflected.

Tuesday, 0100 hrs - it had been a long evening and the sky outside was exceptionally clear. She looked upwards at the shimmering lights that pinpricked the Californian night sky as the familiar sweet, crisp, spicy smell of the pine trees near the balcony gently flavoured the air. As she looked up she saw several shooting stars and could make out the bright starlike Mars with the naked eye.

When she returned to her desk Jess again stared at the screen noting the speed readings. It appeared from the data that Voyager 1 was decelerating again. The data would come through in batches so she wasn't able to see a smooth deceleration, it would instead be shown in large chunks. On this occasion, the data showed the velocity of the spacecraft reducing suddenly from around 38000 mph to around 500 mph. 'Not again' she thought, wondering why these things always happened when she was on her own. Jess stared as the numbers changed and seemed pretty unperturbed, convinced and reassured by Gus and Josh it was just an error. She concluded there was nothing she could do about it at that time and flicked over to Voyager 2 which seemed to be running exactly as expected.

After around five minutes, she got up to stretch her legs and again, walked to the large panoramic window and looked out to the sparse, sun-scarred hills that surround the complex. Coffee in hand she grasped the handle of the glass door with her free hand and with her thumb pushed down on the catch, opening it in one movement the door opened....

WOOSH!

At once the dry hot air rushed into the room and awoke her senses. It was dark but with a full moon she could still see details and for a time she busied herself watching a large brown speckled Owl perched on a branch, 'what a beautiful animal' she thought. It seemed to be intensely looking at something near a bush but no matter how hard she strained her eyes she couldn't see what the target of its focus was. All of a sudden it took to flight, silently closing the gap between it and the bush in the blink of an eye. And then it was over, certainly for its prey, with the Owl flying off into the night. She flicked the last of her coffee over the wall, leaving the coffee grains at the bottom of the cup, closed the door and walked over to the kitchen area, washed her cup out and left it to dry upside down. She walked back to her desk, dragging her feet behind her, wondering if the problems remained.

Jess sat back at her workstation and looked at her screen, noting the speed of Voyager 1 was now only 5 mph. 'Very strange'. She was beginning to think that perhaps this wasn't just an anomaly, having worked there for a short while this was the longest period something like this had gone on for, in fact from what others had said it was very rare for it to go on beyond a day. She decided to screen-record what was happening so she could watch it back with Gus when she handed over to him in the morning. She moved her cursor up to the top of the screen and pressed the red circle.

Suddenly and without warning, one of the instrument panels on her screen flashed red. She stared at it, mouth open.

It was the 'camera on' indicator.

The Voyager 1 spacecraft is equipped with two digital cameras, each 800 x 800 pixels. The cameras on Voyager 2 were switched off in 1989 and Voyager 1's last snap was the now famous 'Pale Blue Dot', a narrow-angle colour image of the solar system which showed the earth as a pale blue dot. A powerful image taken at around 4 billion miles away put into sharp perspective just how small the place where everything we have ever experienced occurred. Voyager 1's cameras were switched off for good 34 minutes after the picture was taken.

Whilst the cameras could still technically function, if they're not frozen, the energy needed to switch them on has long since been used to keep the craft going and communicate with Earth. If they hadn't been switched off they would almost certainly have taken the vital energy needed to keep both Voyagers going. It is believed, therefore, they are no longer functional.

Jess continued to stare open-mouthed. "How?" She said out loud. The camera couldn't just switch itself on, even if it did still work. There was no requirement for them to do so when originally designed. Jess was wondering what to do as the craft started to change direction and sped towards Earth again.......then it appeared to stop. She could see further notifications coming in and went to her inbox to see files being transferred from the spacecraft. "What on earth is going on?" she asked out loud. Jess was overcome as she hovered her mouse over the camera button. Should she press it?

Would she get into trouble if she did? Would it drain the remaining

energy from the craft?

She took a deep breath, then pressed the button.........

4

Peyton Observatory, Princeton University, New Jersey - Tuesday 0100 hrs: Sat on a tall stool, David was writing in his journal on the wooden table adjacent to the 12-inch telescope. Peyton Observatory is located on the roof of Payton Hall and has a large dome on top. 'Well,' he said to himself, 'time to call it a night I think'. With that, he nudged his spectacles up onto his forehead, rubbed his eyes and put his pen down. He picked his satchel up from the floor and placed his journal, pen and now empty leather-wrapped stainless steel flask into it. He smiled as he watched the flask disappear into his satchel, it was a present from his wife, Lizzy. Each Thursday evening she would lovingly fill it with his favourite coffee and send him off to the observatory for a night's work. He loved that. He went through the routine to close the telescope down, replaced the lens cap, parked the telescope in the home position, moved the dome around so the slit was due south (the bad weather tends to come from the north so less chance of water getting in), turned off the telescope and closed the dome. Once complete, he walked out of the room and skipped down the stairs, case in one hand.

Professor David Harris had worked at Princeton for the last ten years. At 37 years of age, he had been married to Lizzie for the last 15 years and they had two children, Ethan and Emily. Lizzie was a teacher at the local high school but still found time to look after the house, children and David. David had a Doctorate in astrophysical sciences from Princeton and had spent most of his adult life in and around the university. David was dedicated to his family and dedicated to science and the exploration of Space. Lizzie allowed him one evening per week where he could go to the observatory and gaze up at the stars like he did the first time he was gifted a telescope for his 12th birthday by his grandmother. Always a gifted mathematician, David suddenly discovered his calling.

David walked down the lane outside the observatory and got onto his pushbike, put his satchel over his shoulder and rode into the night. It was a mild morning with little wind in the air. David was a little cold as he zipped his jacket up and placed his feet on the pedals. He'd had a great evening having spent several hours observing a weather phenomenon on Saturn and its moons. For some reason, he felt inspired and wasn't sure he could wait another week to see more.

The lights were still on at home as David rode his bike through the white wooden garden gate and up the path. The garage was open and David rode straight in, past his tool bench and his spare telescope. He got off his bike, picked it up and hung it on its rack at the back of the garage. As he closed the garage door and walked up to the adjoining door leading to the house, he looked over at the soapbox racer he had been building with his son, Ethan. A Labour of love, they enjoyed working on it together and were looking forward to the father and son soapbox race later in the month, a highlight of the local neighbourhood calendar. He pulled at the cord that operated the light and walked into the house, locking the door behind him. He ambled gently through the dark hallway, trying not to wake the rest of his family, then into the living room where the TV was switched on and Lizzie was asleep on the couch.

He knelt next to her "Hey baby" he whispered in her ear, waking her up gently.

"What time is it?" She asked as she stretched her arms out horizontally over the couch, the arms of her dressing gown rolling down her arms towards her shoulders as she did so.

"Twenty past one" he responded. "You're up for work in a few hours, let's go to bed"

Lizzie hauled herself up and hugged David. She walked past him and out of the door before ascending the stairs. David switched off the TV and followed her up.

"What did you see tonight?" Asked Lizzie as she switched off her bedroom light and turned towards him.

"Too much to tell you when you need some sleep, I'll tell you tomorrow" he switched off his light, kissed her on the forehead and turned to sleep. "Don't forget to pack for New York, I'm really looking forward to our little break away, did mom confirm she's still ok to look after the kids?"

"Yes, go to sleep" responded Lizzie as she playfully tapped him on his shoulder. David looked around and smiled, turned off his bedside light and went to sleep.

NASA Jet Propulsion Laboratory - Tuesday 0130 hrs: Jess sat motionless, mouth open. Her heart beat so fast it caused her to gasp for breath. She was staring at a box on her screen. At the top of the box was a white border with yesterday's date and '0357 hrs' written inside it to signify when the picture was captured. The contents of the box were largely unremarkable but it was what it represented that was significant.

The bottom half of the box was black, nothing could be seen at all, the top half of the box gradually brightened to a smudged white towards the border at the very top. This was the first picture in over 30 years from Voyager 1 and it was completely unexpected. Jess continued to stare at it, unsure what to do next, stomach queasy. There was no protocol for this, no instructions. Should she phone somebody? Should she wait until the morning?

She snapped herself out of her daze, checked the velocity again and noticed it had returned to around 38000 mph. She looked back at the picture again, was that really a new picture? What does it show? She picked up her mobile phone and searched through her contacts, hands shaking, found Gus and pushed the green phone symbol……he would know what to do.

"Jess, this had better be good" he was stern.

"It slowed down again, but"

"Couldn't this have waited?" interrupted Gus.

"The camera Gus, it switched on and took a picture".

There was silence, silence for so long that she thought he'd put the phone down.

"Gus? Gus, did you hear me? It's taken a picture"

"How? That's not possible, are you sure?" he sounded confused

"I'm positive, I've checked and double-checked. What do I do?" She asked

"I'm coming in, you better not be messing with me" and with that, he put the phone down.

Jess put her phone down and looked at the screen again. This was too much, she walked over to the large glass door which led to the balcony outside, pressed the circular metal button and with a whoosh it opened again, welcoming in the hot night air. Jess walked out onto the balcony and looked up at the clear night sky. 'Are all of these nights catching up with me?' she asked herself. The owl was again perched on a small tree a few hundred yards from her, spinning its head around as it followed noises in the surrounding bushes, looking for its next meal.

What if the velocity readings are accurate? How did a camera, that can't turn itself on, switch itself on? Having done that how does it then take a picture? Why does it keep temporarily changing direction and head back in the general direction of the earth? She stood in silence, thinking to herself until the owl flew suddenly off its perch and broke her concentration, snapping her back into consciousness.

Jess went back in through the open door, closing it behind her. She walked over to the coffee machine and made herself a strong coffee then walked back to her workstation. 'I need some answers before Gus comes in' she thought to herself as she re-opened the terminal. She clicked on the picture again, printed a copy and saved it to the JPL's server. Upon looking at the picture again it appeared that the picture was black, not necessarily a surprise, but there was a source of light above the camera. What could this have been? Voyager 1 is not close enough to any sources of light and is now a long way from the sun for it to have been that. This light was close, as in very close. Close enough to cause a real glare that distorted half the picture. Technicians and engineers will be able to work on the picture in the morning and may get more detail but at this time, this is as good as it gets.

Around ten minutes passed and Jess heard the metallic rumble of the main complex gate opening and the low rumble of a car entering the compound. Gus drove a pale blue 1980's VW Beetle which was his treasured possession and Jess recognised the familiar whistle and chirp of the old car as Gus entered the complex. It was in great condition as he cared for that object more than any person, but it was noisy. In truth, if Jess had left the balcony door open, she would probably have heard him leave his house four miles away. He slammed his car door and walked across the car park to the entrance, fumbling around for his access card as he went. Jess felt sick as she heard him walking up the steps and then through the door.

"Well?" An exasperated Gus asked.

"Look at this" replied Jess. She cut straight to the chase, sensing that Gus wasn't in the mood for small talk. Jess wandered back over to her desk with Gus following her, clicked on the screen and highlighted the camera icon, then opened up the picture. There it was, a pretty unremarkable-looking picture as if somebody had overexposed a picture of the night sky. But it wasn't unremarkable, it was very much the opposite, very remarkable indeed. This was a spacecraft hurtling through interstellar space with cameras that were thought to be inoperable. A camera that had switched itself on, something it shouldn't be capable of doing.

"B..but the date" stuttered Gus.

"Yes it's yesterday, obviously it's taken that long to get here. The telemetry corresponds too, it's shown as slowing down at the time the photo was taken"

"I know that Jess……….I just can't believe it". He sat back in the leather office chair and put his right hand on his forehead, allowing gravity to let it slip down as he rubbed his eyes. He sighed……..' this is huge' he whispered to himself.

"I'll get you a coffee, I think I need one too" Jess responded as she walked towards the coffee machine. Gus just stared at the screen, barely able to take in what he had seen. If this was a hoax as some kind of joke from Jess for his dismissive response the previous morning, it was a good one. He checked the file address to be sure and then opened the raw image from within the main Voyager program. This was what she said, an image from interstellar space, the first glimpse ever seen by human eyes.

"What do we do now Gus?" Quizzed Jess as she walked back towards him with two mugs of fresh coffee. She placed one on a coaster next to the computer and fished a second coaster out of her draw with her now free hand. She placed the second mug down and grabbed a second chair from behind her before sitting at it, staring at the screen. Gus didn't answer, he just stared at the screen. It was now closer to 0230 hrs and they were still several hours from the next working day.

As they both stared at the screen......it happened again.

First, Voyager 1 decelerated to 500 mph, then it changed direction and headed back towards Earth again. Gus felt his stomach sink as he watched. Whilst he didn't disbelieve Jess, there's nothing like seeing it as it happens, to focus your thoughts. A couple of minutes later, as quickly as it started, it stopped and resumed its original course and velocity. The colour drained from Gus's face as he sat there with his mouth open, he turned to Jess and opened his mouth but no words came out.

"I know, right?" Said Jess as a broad smile crossed her face. She picked up her mug and put her hands around it as if warming them. "Do we need to contact anybody, Gus?"

"And tell them what Jess? No, we need to continue to monitor this and record what we see. We are going to be bombarded with hundreds of questions when everybody comes in, we need to be prepared. Have you started to record your observations?"

"Not yet, it's all been a bit of a blur, to be honest"

"That's ok, start now, record exactly what happened and when and I will start doing the same, believe me this is going to get very real when everybody else comes in later."

"Ok, we need to keep an eye out too, in case something else happens" replied Jess.

As they both settled down to type out their observations, the reassuring beep of the two spacecraft continued in the background.

5

Jet Propulsion Laboratory - Tuesday 0830 hrs. The coffee machine was working hard to keep up with the number of people now filling the room, filling the stale air-conditioned air with the smell of fresh coffee beans. Debra, Brian and several others were now in the office looking quizzically at screens as Gus and Jess enthusiastically told them of their observations overnight.

Brian Stevens was another senior researcher and had been at JPL for about ten years, a lover of classical music, his true passion was playing the Cello and he spent most of his free time playing for the local community orchestra.

"Listen" demanded Debra, the room quietened "I've got a conference call with other project leads at nine-thirty, I need a really clear picture by then as this is going to blow their minds. Have we considered switching the camera back on ourselves?" Debra was usually an ocean of calm but this was pressure and she had reacted to it.

"Yes we tried that" responded Gus, "but it's not possible, you can see that there is not enough energy to start them. It makes what happened all the more puzzling."

"I need some kind of explanation or at least a hypothesis to take to this meeting, I can't just go there and say I don't know what's happened or why, we will be the laughing stock. You have both known about this longer than the rest of us, what are your thoughts?"

"Well," Jess spoke quietly with Gus staring at her nervously, wondering what she was going to say. "Well we've ruled out error, everything seems to be working as it should. I suppose it could be the environment which has caused it to malfunction in a very specific way. It's hostile out there and we have nothing as far away as Voyager 1, who knows what that can do? The other theory is........"

"Go on" Debra cut the silence brutally, she was impatient.

"Well, it could be a third party, something out there that has done this. Something either from this world or another" Debra sat on the edge of the desk, looking intently at Jess. Sensing this wasn't enough and being uncomfortable with silence Jess felt compelled to speak again, "We simply don't know what's out there and I don't see how we could move this spacecraft around at those speeds, humans that is, so I wonder if it's not humans doing it"

There was an uncomfortable silence. Debra stood up, walked over to the large screen near the window, turned back and engaged Jess, "I am not going to a meeting with some of the most senior and experienced scientists on this planet and telling them that goddamn aliens have taken control of Voyager 1.......I'll be taken away and put in hospital!!" She let out a deep breath, realising that the stress of the situation was bringing the worst out in her, walked back across the office and sat on her chair. "I'm sorry Jess, that was uncalled for. Can you give me what you've got I'm gonna have to just admit we are puzzled. I need you all on this though so this is the priority. By the way, how is Voyager 2 looking?"

"No change" responded Jess, her characteristic buoyant outlook having returned following the apology. "We'll continue to monitor both".

"No Jess, you need some sleep, I need you at your best for tonight although you won't be on your own for once you'll have some company!"

With that, Debra stood up and walked out to the balcony door and the warm Californian air. She rummaged around in her pocket and took her vape out. She was stressed which was unusual for her. She genuinely couldn't explain what had happened or why and it was a situation she wasn't used to. She stood, vape in hand, looking across the scorched ground at a small lizard scooting around the wall that adjoined the building. 'What is going on?' She asked herself.

Jess got into her car and turned the key in the ignition. The car radio sparked into life with a phone-in about a water shortage and drought and whether California should ban water sprinklers. 'What on earth am I going to come into tonight?' She wondered. She didn't need to wonder in truth, Gus would be messaging her all day whilst she slept. As she drove out through the large metal gate, the Californian sun started to beat down on her, she lowered her window to let some fresh air in. It seemed like the same morning she had experienced many times before, driving home to bed after a long night at the JPL but it wasn't, and it would never be the same again.......

Debra walked into one of the conference rooms and logged into the main computer, she was joined by a couple of colleagues who acknowledged her but were already mid conversation about one of their recent vacations. Debra wasn't listening, she moved to her remote panel and pressed the link to the meeting. They were in, one by one the faces lit up the screen, all familiar and all about to get some news they weren't expecting.

"Morning all, I hope we are well, nearly the weekend!" Debra was used to the Director of the Jet Propulsion Laboratory, Jennifer Strongs' commentary on where they were in the week. She had tried to contact Jennifer earlier in the morning to pre-warn her of her upcoming revelation but without success. With over 6000 employees and a plethora of projects of national and world importance, the Director ran a tight ship. "OK, before we start, is there any exceptional business this morning?" This part of the meeting was usually reserved for minor technical or personnel issues, Jennifer wasn't expecting what came next.

"Yes" coughed Debra, "I have something".

"Go on, Debra" responded Jennifer.

"It's hard to know where to start to be honest. A couple of nights ago we recorded some unusual readings from Voyager 1. As you all know it is around 15 billion miles away and at a current velocity of around 38000 mph." There were nods around the conference in agreement. "Well, a couple of nights ago the spacecraft appeared to experience several sudden and unexplained changes of velocity, ranging from significant reductions to what appeared to be a complete change of direction with Voyager heading back towards Earth. After a short period, it changed back and returned its original velocity and course." There was silence. Debra felt suddenly very alone despite being amongst a number of people.

"How is this the first I'm hearing about this Debra." Asked Jennifer, slightly stern but also perplexed.

"That's not all Jennifer. We assumed the readings were an error and the engineers were in the process of making contact with Voyager to better understand what had happened and how. Obviously, this takes a couple of days so I was waiting for this before I came to you. Last night the strange readings started again, very similar with sudden reductions in velocity, a change of course but this time it was different......"

"Different how, Debra?"

"Well.......I'm just going to share a picture with you" Debra moved her cursor over a square with an arrow on it, pressed the mouse button and clicked on the picture she was about to share. She pressed the button

"What on earth is that?" asked Jennifer.

"This is a photo taken by Voyager 1, two nights ago. It would appear that the camera switched itself back on and took a photograph. It seems that there is a light source towards the top of the picture and the rest of it is black. I've followed the file pathways and it's been checked a number of times and it's the real deal. It's the first picture in over 30 years and I have absolutely no explanation as to how or why it happened. I was handed this a few hours ago and I currently have a team working on some hypothesis but, effectively you now know what I know."

Nothing......silence. Debra sat back in her seat, tipped her head back, pulled her shoulder-length hair back and tied it into a ponytail. She was nervous and her childhood tendency to play with her hair when nervous had made an unexpected return.

"Ok, This is kinda hard to process right now. So you are telling me that Voyager 1 is currently out of control in interstellar space? Is this some kind of joke?"

"No Jennifer, it's not a joke. This is serious and everything I've told you has been checked and double-checked to the extent we can given the limits we have to work within."

Jennifer sat back, nudged her spectacles onto her forehead with her hand, and rubbed her eyes. "Right, Debra we need to talk. The rest of you, can you get me your resource returns soonest please, I need to know what you can give towards this and I need your most experienced problem solvers please, no interns. I want the circle of knowledge on this to be tight, very tight. None of you are to talk outside the Voyager lab about this and those that have knowledge are to be spoken to immediately and told the same. If I find anybody has leaked on this, they'll be lucky to get a job teaching elementary physics. Debra, I'm coming over now, I'll see you in about 30 minutes." Jennifer had planned to work from home all day but she knew her presence was needed. She was suddenly very focused, she

68

loved a challenge and thrived on pressure, this was just her kind of challenge.

Jennifer ended the conference call and set about gathering her things before going into the laboratory. She moved through the house on automatic pilot, scooping up her laptop, keys and water bottle before walking out to her car, opening the door and sitting on her boiling-hot leather driver's seat. Jennifer liked the finer things in life and her black Porsche was certainly one of those, she slotted the key into its cassette, put her foot on the break and pressed the glowing start button. As she drove out of her electric gates and signalled to pull onto the road, she could hardly have imagined what the day would bring, but her nervous energy was positively driving her on.

Back at JPL, Gus was busy reading through the telemetry from Voyager 1, lost in his thoughts. He had a flat white latte in his left hand and, pen in his right hand, was busy marking off numbers on a large blue sheet of paper. There was a quiet hum in the room as various experts, drafted in from across the JPL, sought to understand what they were dealing with. The large lab' had room enough for 50 people and that capacity was now close to being exceeded. In the background was the large double screen, 75 inches in size. On the left screen were the figures pertaining to Voyager 1, on the right Voyager 2. Both sent back figures regularly on velocity and track, albeit from 24 hours or so earlier. Most eyes were not on the screens as they read through sheets of figures and their own screens with mathematical equations so complex they were unfathomable to all but the most proficient and talented scientists. But still, despite some of the greatest minds focused on this one issue, nobody had a reasonable explanation for what they were reading and as Jennifer walked in there was barely an acknowledgement from others in the room.

"Where's Debra?" Jennifer asked in a slightly raised voice. As she looked over the sea of people she saw a couple of hands motioning in the direction of the conference room door in the corner. She walked across the room, barely looking at anything apart from the door she had targeted, tapping on the glass as she arrived. "Hi Debra, may I?" She motioned towards the empty chair opposite Debra's. The rest of the room was empty with Debra using the room as a quiet space to gather her thoughts and theories. As the senior scientist working on the Voyager programme, she felt responsible for what was happening and professionally embarrassed that she had little or no explanation as to what had happened. Debra prided herself on being the go-to person when there were any decisions around voyager, any question, any confusion. Having worked on the project nearly her entire adult life she was in an uncomfortable place for her.

"Of course, nice to see you" replied Debra, she sounded tired.

"Can you give me an update?" Asked Jennifer.

"Sure, although we're not much further forward. I guess the most significant update is we now have a full team working on this, thank you for helping me pull that together. There have been no further anomalistic readings from Voyager and we are just pouring through the data."

"Sure…….Debra, I'm not going to be able to keep this within JPL for long. This is a significant development and I am going to have to brief NASA fully at some point. I don't need to point out how important it is that we have some kind of explanation as to what has happened when I do, do I?"

"This is my life's work, my entire professional reputation is on the line here. You don't need to put me under pressure, I will ensure that if there is a rational explanation, I'll get it."

Before Jennifer had the opportunity to respond, they heard loud chatter coming from the adjacent room. As they burst through the door they were greeted by every scientist in the room crowded around the large screens. Gus turned around, "it's happening again" he called. As they walked quickly towards the screen it soon became clear what he meant, but this time it was different.

6

Princeton University, New Jersey, Tuesday, 11 am. David Harris was in his office at Princeton, reading through emails and deleting the non-urgent ones. David received so many emails he never got to the end of them and his philosophy was, if they're that important I'm sure they'll send another. It was a small office but big enough to fit his desk, a large table and several chairs, he often used it for tutorials as he found it to be a more intimate and supportive environment than one of the large characterless classrooms others use. It was untidy, reflecting the disorganised state of his mind, something he would never get away with at home as Lizzy wouldn't allow it.

He sat with his phone next to him, with Bach playing in the background to relax him. Whilst he stared at his screen, deleting another departmental newsletter, his mind wandered back to Saturn and the weather patterns he had seen the previous evening. 'They were spectacular' he thought and knew once again that he wouldn't be able to wait another week before he saw them again. As great as the telescope at the observatory was, it still appeared as not much more than a blur, but tonight was set to be clearer. He decided he would bargain with Lizzie to get another session, but what could he offer? Their weekend in New York started the following day and he had taken time off work so they could get away early, he had also booked a meal at her favourite Italian Restaurant in Hells Kitchen. Perhaps if he told her that was the plan she would be more inclined to let him out again that evening?

As he deleted another spam email pertaining to be from the IRS, he had decided to do what it took to get out. He stood, turned and looked out of the window behind his desk, the tree outside his office window was just beginning to turn and reveal its fall foliage. He loved this time of the year and had done since he was a child, Halloween was always a big occasion and he was now ensuring his children had the same experience, costumes and candy aplenty over the period. He smiled to himself as he picked his jacket up from the back of his chair and put it on before grabbing his leather briefcase and leaving the office. No more lectures that day and no need to be in the office.

As he walked out of the door and down the hall, he bumped into another professor, James Willis. "Hi James, how are you?"

"Very well thanks Professor Harris" James was always formal but, despite that they shared a passionate interest in the gas giants, Jupiter and Saturn. "Are you off?"

"Yes, end of the week for me, off to New York for a few days with Lizzie. Have you been watching Saturn lately? I've been watching some really unusual movements, well best I can, worth a look if you get a chance. It's really hard from this distance to figure out whether it's from the planet or one of the moons. Looking at where it appears to come from I'd say it's Titan."

"Really? I'll have a look" not a man of many words and certainly not gifted with the ability to small talk, with that they went their separate ways.

Titan is the second largest moon in the solar system behind Jupiter's moon Ganymede and is around 50% larger than Earth's moon and larger than the planet Mercury. Both Voyager 1 and Voyager 2 flew close by to examine Titan in the early 1980s but it was covered in haze at the time. It has since been visited by a number of probes including Huygens, which landed on its surface in 2005. Titan has an inhospitable environment but, despite this, many have theorised that life could exist on this outpost far from the Earth as it has an atmosphere not dissimilar to Earth, indeed humans wouldn't need a suit to protect them if it wasn't so cold, just an oxygen mask. Life, however, is still a far-fetched theory with our current understanding of biology.

Jet Propulsion Laboratory - The telemetry on Voyager 2 was showing significant variation very similar to its sister spacecraft the previous nights. Silence gripped the room as the direction of Voyager 2 changed and it appeared to be moving back towards Earth with the distance ticking downwards. Gus felt vindicated as in the back of his mind he worried that others thought he and Jess had exaggerated what Jess had seen before, in fact, he wondered that himself. Silence slowly settled across the room like a soft blanket as some of the greatest minds in space science processed what they'd seen.

A short time later Debra and Jennifer were back in the side room talking. "So, what are the chances that an anomaly has randomly occurred on both spacecraft? One I can see, but both of them?" Jennifer was puzzled and was genuinely hoping Debra had an answer.

"Well they are identical.........but no, it's unlikely. All I'd say is they are in uncharted territory. Both are so far away now that they are likely to encounter turbulence and objects we have previously been unaware existed. I mean, that's the point of this mission to a certain extent, isn't it? Listen, I think if we get too hung up on having an explanation for this early on we will be setting ourselves up to fail. We need to go public and we need to be honest. We also need to ensure we are monitoring both spacecraft 24/7, I'll ensure we have the cover in place." Debra had recovered from her earlier uncertainty and was now feeling much more confident.

"OK, I'm going to brief the administrator of NASA" responded Jennifer. "Are you ok to brief with me?"

"Sure" responded Debra.

Jet Propulsion Laboratory - 1800 hrs, Tuesday - Jess walked into the lab and noticed immediately how busy it was. There were still dozens of scientists pouring over data and Gus, who had been up since one that morning, greeted her as she came in. "Look at what you've done!!" he joked, smiling at Jess. "Seriously Jess, you won't be on your own tonight, there's going to be a big team on and you'll be assisting".

Jess was chewing gum and taking her water out of her bag "Sure" she smiled back. "You need to go home Gus, you've been up so long and you need to sleep. I'll keep you updated so don't worry, you won't miss anything."

Gus smiled again and gathered his things, said goodbye to some of the others and then walked out to his beloved Beetle. Jess walked over to Brian to ask how she could assist. Once briefed, she went over to the coffee machine to pour out her first coffee of the evening.

New Jersey, Tuesday evening - He succeeded! David had been given an evening pass to the telescope from Lizzie, in no small part because of the restaurant reservation for New York, and was on his bike on his way back to the Peyton Observatory. It was a still and clear night, he had an excited knot in his stomach as he rode along the well-lit paths, wondering what lay ahead that night. By the time he had arrived at the observatory, the light was beginning to fade and the lights of the main building were switched on. He walked through the main door and up the steps to the telescope, using his access card to get in. As he looked at the wonderfully crafted and well-loved telescope, he felt his mobile phone vibrating in his front pocket. 'Oh Lizzie, I've only just got here!' He muttered to himself, assuming his wife wanted to confirm some of the arrangements for the forthcoming weekend. As he turned his phone around and saw the alert, he realised he had been rather harsh as it was not her at all, it was his colleague James.

"Get to a telescope and look at Saturn then call me!!" The message read.

James wasn't known for drama at all and was a very even-mannered fellow. 'Seems like he's seen what I did' David thought to himself.

David checked the coordinates and directed the telescope towards the giant ringed gas planet. He needn't have bothered checking the coordinates though, something unusual was happening and may even have been visible with the naked eye had he not been in a trance on his way to the observatory. As he looked at Saturn, he could see what looked like a thick blue lightning bolt going from just beyond the planet, out beyond Saturn until it faded in the distance. Having double-checked the coordinates it looked like the light was coming from Titan again. He picked up his mobile phone and called his colleague

"David, are you watching what I'm watching?" James was uncharacteristically informal.

"Yes, what on earth is it?" Spluttered David.

"It looks like an electrical energy charge but it's not going to the planet so I don't think it's related to Saturn's atmosphere, how does it go beyond Saturn without reacting to the gravitational pull of the planet? Theoretically, that should be impossible" responded James. Both men sounded like excited teenagers who had just peered through a telescope for the first time, not two eminent professors from one of the foremost universities in the world.

As they started to theorise whether the source was Titan or somewhere else and stopped on Titan, other astronomers were beginning to report on social media this bright phenomenon occurring near Saturn. The noise on social media began to increase to a crescendo with mainstream media picking it up and then NASA following suit. As the mighty James Webb Space Telescope started to collect data, the Jet Propulsion Laboratory, which sends and receives signals from the James Webb hadn't yet put the two biggest issues they were dealing with together. It would be several days before the images would be processed from James Webb but what was clear was that this was a phenomenon never before recorded. The bolt of light looked similar to the one often used to destroy planets in science fiction movies, but this didn't seem to be destroying anything, it was just a bolt stretching from the area of Titan, out to deep space.

JPL - Jess was listening to Brian try to explain what was happening to the two Voyager spacecraft. He seemed less convinced than most that the changes in velocity and direction were down to a third party. He was using the whiteboard in the lab and a board marker to draw a basic map of the universe in three dimensions, showing the sun powering through space and the planets whizzing around at various angles.

"Now what's to say that, once you get beyond the pull of our star, those orbits don't become more erratic? I mean, obviously, they weren't orbiting anything, but you get where I'm coming from.

Now, whilst we think that, on a few occasions the distance between earth and the spacecraft has reduced it doesn't necessarily mean they are coming towards earth as such."

Suddenly the screen started beeping and flashing and everybody's attention focused on the giant screens again. Both Voyager spacecraft were losing velocity again, for the first time, simultaneously. They sat in stunned silence as Jess walked over to the keyboard, she had seen this before and was no longer shocked by these activities. A couple of minutes later, the distances from Earth on both screens started to reduce, producing a gasp from more than one person in the room.

The camera icon on Voyager 2 became active, flashing on the screen.

"Shall I?" Asked Jess.

Brian nodded, The Voyager 2 camera had been inactive for even longer than the one on Voyager 1, having been last used a year earlier in 1989. Brian nodded, Jess pressed the button, there were gasps once more. Jess saved the picture and then maximised it on a third large QLED screen.

The picture was largely black, similar to the previous night, but this time there was a white circle in the centre of the screen. It appeared to be an electric blue and wasn't a perfect circle but had what appeared to be bolts of electricity arcing off to the sides. Before anybody could say a word, the camera icon on Voyager 1 became active and started flashing indicating that it had been switched on. There were gasps around the room again as once more, Jess clicked on the picture, saved it and moved it to the large screen. Brian gasped

"Oh my…….."

Wednesday 0200 hrs - David left the observatory and started his journey home. Largely unaware of the significance of the events he had witnessed, he was nevertheless brimming with excitement at having witnessed a weather phenomenon like no other. By comparison, the weather on his part of the earth was pretty tame that evening. A relatively cool and clear night, it had been the perfect night to watch the show Saturn and Titan had put on earlier. As he cycled down the lane, the leaves from the trees fell gently around him like snow, spinning into a gentle circle. He was excited about their trip to New York and looked forward to sharing what he had seen that evening with Lizzie.

JPL, California - The room was silent. The picture from Voyager 1 was the most impactful yet. Everybody in the room stared wide-eyed at the new photograph, disbelief was widespread. Unlike the other pictures this one looked like it contained something living, the contours were clear and it appeared to glisten, albeit the picture was in black and white until they ran filters through it. Towards the centre of the picture was a very pale circle. If this was a creature of some kind, it was staring at them from deep space. A cold chill ran through Jess as the hairs on her arms stood to attention. Brian dragged his eyes away from the screen momentarily and said quietly

"I need somebody to run a filter through this photograph soonest please".

The enormous nature of this discovery was evident to all. Brian stroked his chin nervously as he looked back at the team, tears welling in his eyes.

"Well, we appear to have made contact with extraterrestrial life," he said, voice wavering with emotion. "Jennifer and Debra will need to be briefed and then the President through the Administrator. Jess, contact Debra and tell her what's happened, we need to move on this quickly".

Jess scuttled off towards the balcony, through the doors and then outside. She took her mobile out, hands shaking as adrenaline coursed through her veins, and called Debra.

Debra had been expecting a call at some point and had only left work to make sure her dog could get outside and to make arrangements for him over the coming days, she knew this wasn't the end of this story. She barely acknowledged Jess as she briefed her, it didn't sink in, she collected her things and made her way next door with her dog. Her neighbours had agreed to look after him for a few days though they had no idea what was happening.

Debra opened her car door and stepped inside, pulling away as the automatic seatbelt pulled her back into her seat. As she walked back into the office a short while later, the image from Voyager 1 was being studied having just been enhanced and colourised/filtered. The result was now being displayed on the main screen and it was now clearer than ever this was an encounter with extraterrestrial life. The light-coloured disc in the middle of the screen was actually pale blue and appeared textured, almost like a close-up of knitted wool. The skin, if it was indeed that, was glistening from an external light source. The biggest surprise of all was its colour, bright red and black. On earth, bright colours tend to be a warning to other animals to stay away and some of the most venomous animals on the planet are the brightest. Why was this creature so bright? Who was it warning?

7

New York City, Wednesday, 17:00 - David and Lizzy drove through the Lincoln Tunnel towards Manhattan Island. No matter how many times they made that journey it was still awe-inspiring to see the giant buildings towering over the skyline. They negotiated the busy city streets, each set of traffic lights taking an age to change, before parking the car and then walking into the hotel to check-in. They had already decided that they would go to Central Park first, as they always did, on their way to dinner. Whilst Lizzie knew David had made a reservation for dinner, she had no idea where she was going, she loved a surprise so she didn't press him too hard. It was almost as if they hadn't arrived until they visited the iconic green space and they felt like they'd investigated every inch of the giant park over the years.

The Hotel was amongst the finest in the Country, let alone the City, and David and Lizzie were excited to see what lay beyond the giant revolving gold doors. As they navigated the doors and entered the main hotel lobby they were immediately tantalized by the fragrances of fresh flowers mixed with carefully placed diffusers and luxury oils to create a sense of opulence. They walked across the shiny white marbled floor towards the main reception, a sweeping solid dark wooden desk and a perfectly presented member of staff behind it, completely unflustered by the chaotic activity around him.

"Sir, Madam, welcome to the hotel, how may I help you today?"

"Reservation for David Harris"

David responded to the immaculately turned-out receptionist's question. They went through the formalities and David handed over his credit card before they were given the swipe card for their room.

David picked up his suitcase and pulled the handle proud of the main unit, locking it into place with a click. He then walked over towards the shiny gold elevator, Lizzie beside him, and waited for their carriage up into the bowels of the hotel. Once they reached their destination, the elevator spat them out onto a thick plush carpeted corridor and a short while later they stood outside their hotel room door as David rested the card against the card reader.

The gold-coloured plate on the door had a small light which turned from red to green and made a 'bleep' as the door opened. As they walked into a pristine room, David took a deep breath in through his nose, he loved the smell of freshly polished wood. As they walked further into the room it opened out to reveal a giant bed and an even larger TV. Next to the window was a small round table with a beautiful bunch of flowers, a bottle of champagne and a metal bucket of ice.

"David!!"

Lizzie had a smile as wide as her face as she turned to her husband. She planted a huge kiss on his lips then picked up the bunch of flowers, tipped them to one side and read the note attached.

"To my darling Lizzie. Thank you for the privilege of being able to call you my wife x"

She placed them back down and hugged him. David was so grateful for the opportunity to see what had been happening on Saturn these last few nights and she needed to understand how important it was to him. The room was drenched in dark wood which matched the desk in reception and was fully deserving of its five-star status. They were delighted with the quality and looked forward to spending a few nights there. Located on the 19th floor, the hotel also benefited from a view of Central Park unrivalled by most.

"Are you hungry?" Asked David as he looked across the green park in the middle of the city.

"I will be soon, can we go to Capzzi's? I have been craving their Lasagna since we decided to come here, it's been far too long hasn't it?"

Capzzi's, on the Western edge of Central Park overlooking it from an adjacent street, had long been a favourite of David and Lizzie's. It had been the location of one of their first dates when David wanted to show Lizzie his love of Italy and they had come to New York City for a day trip. Ever since it was the restaurant they'd visit first every time they went there, they rarely missed a visit. They always chose the same table and asked the waiter to light the candle as David had done on that first date.

David and Lizzie met in High School where they were both enthusiastic members of the science club. Their relationship began as friends and they were rarely out of each other's company. They attended most of the same classes and David would often help Lizzie with her homework as he was by far the more academically talented of the two. David was in love with Lizzie from the start, but Lizzie didn't share those feelings, seeing them as friends and no more. They attended different colleges with David going to Princeton and Lizzie to Boston University. Distance helped Lizzie realise her true feelings for her best friend as she couldn't get him out of her mind. David can still remember their first kiss outside the front of his house one evening. As he held her close, gazing deeply into her eyes, he wanted the moment to never end.

"I've already booked our usual table, you didn't think I would forget did you?" David smiled in that knowing way, quietly pleased with himself.

"Haha, of course not, but a lady needs to check. I'll freshen up and grab a quick shower, change then I'm ready" She headed off into the bathroom and David continued to stare out of the window across Central Park, happy he was there, still replaying the previous few night's activities in his mind.

Long Island City, New York: "It's time to get up Doug!" Doug Jackson had lived in Long Island City for over 30 years and loved how it effortlessly combined fast city life with quiet suburbia. He lived there with his wife Jackie and their two grown-up children, Troy and Madison. Alongside the four human members of the family, there were Doug's other babies, his five cats. Doug loved his cats and referred to them as his furry children.

"Ok, I'm coming, I'll be glad when I don't have to do this any more Jack. I'm getting far too old to work this late." Doug rolled out of bed and stretched his arms high as he gently eased himself back to consciousness. He picked his well-worn spectacles up from his bedside table, blew the dust off the lenses, then balanced them on his nose whilst he hooked them around his ears.

"Have you fed the cats, Jack?" Doug shouted down the stairs as he balanced himself against the wooden bannister.

"My god Doug, they're the first thing you think about, aren't they? If only you loved me as much as them" she joked as she shouted back up the stairs at her beloved husband. Doug was getting ready for his night shift at the local power plant and this exchange was now almost a ritual between the two of them.

Manhattan: "This place just never stops does it?" David was blinking as his eyes readjusted to the daylight. "We've got an hour until our reservation, it's only a thirty-minute walk so shall we skip the cab?"

"Yeh, why not" responded Lizzie, "I love to breathe in this city, it makes me feel like I'm here, you know?"

David glanced across at his wife "Yeh, yeh I do" he responded, smiling. They started to walk up towards Central Park, passing some typical New York eateries on the way. "I'm almost tempted, aren't you?" Asked David as they walked past a New York pizza shop selling slices of New York's finest for $2.50. The smell reached out from the green, white and red awning which adorned the front of the shop, sneaking up their nostrils and tantalizing their taste buds.

"You do remember how big the portions are at Capzzi's don't you? I'm so hungry but that would be such a huge mistake" Lizzie chuckled as she squeezed David's hand.

As they reached the edge of Central Park, David stopped suddenly, he loved the park and just wanted to breathe in the smell of the freshly cut grass. He noticed a small grey squirrel sitting on the side wall which marks the perimeter of that part of the park. It was nibbling furiously at a candied nut it had either found or been given.

He continued to watch as the little animal pushed its treasure into the corner of its mouth as a large crow approached it, then scuttled up a tree. 'I'm glad life as a human isn't that hectic' David reflected as he continued his journey towards the restaurant. Lizzie and David were deep in conversation as the full-on hustle and bustle of New York City went on around them. So engrossed were they in each other they couldn't hear the cacophony around them as New Yorkers went about their business.

Long Island City: "What are you watching?" Asked Jackie as she placed a cold glass of lemon iced tea on the table in front of Doug. He was sat back on the couch with Freda, one of his cats, on his lap.

"Oh it's just a documentary about Mars rovers, it's hard to believe we've sent these vehicles all the way to another planet, absolutely fascinating"

"You really won't struggle to find things to do with your time when you do retire, will you? Did you call your HR department for your final pension quote like I asked you to? If you don't get that you won't be going anywhere"

"I'm going to do it today Jackie, I promise" replied Doug as he picked up his ice-cool beverage and took the first sip.

"Hmmm, I'll believe it when I see it, you'll never retire" She responded as a smile crept across her face.

Manhattan: "We have a reservation for Harris." Said David to the immaculately dressed Maitre D'.

"Certainly sir, if you'll follow me please?" He proceeded to guide the couple through the busy restaurant, dodging waiters with trays stacked high with tasty Italian food, before he came to a halt at an empty table next to a window overlooking the road and then Central Park beyond. This was the table they had reserved on numerous occasions previously and David had ensured they would sit there when he had phoned the Restaurant to make the reservation.

"May I introduce you to Marco who will be looking after you this evening?" he announced as he beckoned forward their waiter for the evening. Tall with black slicked-back hair, olive-skinned and wearing black trousers, a white shirt and a white apron draped down from his waist, he was every part the quintessential Italian Waiter.

"Good evening sir, madam. Can I fetch you a drink whilst you look through the menu?" Asked Marco.

"Yes please, do you still sell the Cantina Terlano Vorberg Pinot Bianco Riserva?" Although he sounded like it in that moment, David was by no means a wine connoisseur, he had been recommended the fine white wine by a previous sommelier and they had treated themselves to a bottle at every return visit.

"Of course sir, and may I say, that's a fine choice" Marco responded as he gently opened the menus, first in front of Lizzie and then in front of David.

In truth, they didn't need the menus as they would both choose exactly the same dish that had delighted their palates on every previous occasion. They enjoyed looking through the menu though, it prolonged their time there and was part of the experience, and who knows, there may be something new.

Long Island City: Doug took his lunch box, lovingly packed with his favourite food by Jackie, from the kitchen and picked up his backpack from the floor near the door as he made his way out. He selected his keys from the small wooden key rack on the wall to the left of the front door and put them into his left pocket.

"I'm off honey" Doug hollered as he opened the door.

"Wait, I'm coming" replied Jackie as she walked out of their bedroom, ran down the stairs and wrapped her arms around him before planting a kiss on his left cheek. "I love you babe, take care"

"Take care? I'm going to work Jack, like I've done every night for years, I'll see you again in a few hours" He smiled back.

"I know" she replied.

Doug walked through the door and in no time at all was breathing in the cool evening. It was a clear and fresh night and as he looked up he marveled at the spectacular canvas of natural art above him as stars glistened like fine jewels.

Manhattan: "Thank you David, that was amazing" said Lizzie as they walked out of the restaurant. She placed her hand through his arm and they stepped out into the clear evening air. "This was exactly what we needed, I never tire of that place, the food was exquisite as always."

"It really was good wasn't it? Shall we walk back to the hotel?" Asked David hopefully. He was hoping to catch a glimpse of the night sky as they walked to see if there was any sign of the weather phenomenon he had previously spotted near Saturn. He had concluded that the chances of seeing anything with the naked eye was slim but he couldn't resist another look.

"Sure, why not, it'll be romantic." Lizzie smiled broadly as they stepped off the sidewalk and crossed the road towards Central Park.

A brisk walk and thirty minutes later they had returned to the hotel. David was disappointed not to have seen the spectacular light show he had seen on previous evenings', concluding that perhaps it was just not viewable with the naked eye. He was tempted to text his colleague who he knew would be 'with telescope' that evening but reflected that perhaps this would be a step too far for Lizzie and he didn't wish to spoil what had been a perfect evening thus far.

As they walked into the hotel room, the lights automatically activated, illuminating the luscious interior. David walked over to the window as Lizzie removed her shoes and sat on the bed to rest her feet.

"That's a relief," said Lizzie as she let out a sigh. She fell back on the bed and stared up at the ceiling as she relaxed for the first time that day.

Over at the window, David glanced across the top of the trees towards the sheep meadow, a large lush green towards the west of the park. He could see a couple of people strolling across enjoying the ambience when all of a sudden he heard a loud crack, he looked up and could see a bright light moving at pace across the sky, arcing downwards towards the park. He looked at Lizzie's terrified face and grabbed her hand.

"I'm going into the park, looks like that's going to land there."

They sped out of the door as Lizzie fought to pull on her slip-on shoes then ran down the back staircase and onto the street. By now they could see a plume of smoke rising from the direction of the sheep meadow. There didn't seem to be a huge amount of fuss as New Yorkers busied themselves with themselves and he easily made his way to the sheep meadow where he was greeted by a small crater with smoke emanating and a crowd beginning to form.

They both stood and stared into the pit at what seemed like smouldering metal.

"What is it, David?" Quizzed Lizzie.

David was perplexed......it clearly wasn't a rock, it was metallic and looked completely different. It measured around 1 meter across and looked like twisted black metal, David felt sure it had burned through the atmosphere and wondered if it was an old satellite that had fallen out of orbit, unlikely given the ferocity and intensity of atmospheric pressure it would have been subjected to. The buckled metal was barely distinguishable and still far too hot to touch. By stark contrast, the temperature of the air around the crash site had dropped suddenly, with what appeared to be a frost now around the Sheep Meadow. As the air began to scream with sirens, David decided this was his only chance to explore this object and decided to wait for the Police and other emergency services to arrive. He decided to stick around and planned to explain to the authorities he was a scientist and might be able to help identify the object. What did he have to lose?

As he waited he noticed the leaves on the surrounding trees rustling, 'strange' he thought 'There's no wind today'. He watched as the trees rustled one after another, almost like the ripple made when you throw a stone into the middle of a lake. He thought no more of it and explained his plan to Lizzie. Lizzie seemed unsettled, without the scientific acumen of her husband she was relying on her instinct, and her instinct was telling her something was wrong, very wrong.

A number of police and fire vehicles arrived and their passengers sped quickly to put 'scene tape' around the crash site.

"Sir, I need you to move back behind the tape" an officious NYPD Officer was controlling an excitable crowd which had now formed around the impact crater.

"Sir, I won't warn you again"

"Officer, my name is David and I'm a scientist from Princeton University, my expertise is space. Please, don't make me leave, I think I can help you. Whatever that is, I'm sure it came from beyond our atmosphere, I might know what it is." David was being a little liberal with the truth as he had no clue what it was.

The Officer looked David up and down, behind him officers in thick hazard suits were already examining the wreckage, trying to find something that would identify its origin.

JPL, California - "Turn that up!!" Instructed Brian, pointing at one of the screens in the Jet Propulsion Laboratory. The news was broadcasting a breaking story, an unidentified object had crashed into Central Park and the news helicopter was broadcasting images from above the impact crater. As the volume increased, the team listened in intently:

"No Ron, there are no markers that we can see, it does appear to be metal but that's all we know for sure. They've watered it to try and cool it down and it looks like officers with cutting equipment are going to try and pull it apart."

"What is going on?" Brian asked himself out loud.

Jess felt her phone vibrating in her back pocket and picked it up…..it was a message from Gus that simply proclaimed "WTF???" She smiled and replied, "I know, right?" She returned her phone to her pocket and carried on watching the footage. As the officers cut through the wreckage, it remained largely unidentifiable until….

New York - "We got something!!" Suddenly activity increased around the crater and a man in a black suit walked past the uniforms to one of the officers in a hazard suit. He passed the smart-suited man what looked like part of a sheet of metal in the shape of a triangle but with one of the edges curved. As it was handed over to the man in the suit, David could see light reflecting off it. David took his phone out, pointed it at the object and opened his camera app, he zoomed in on the object and took a photo.

Upon reviewing the photo David thought it looked yellow and he could see some lines on the front. He again appealed to the officer near him

"Come on man, just tell him who I am and let me have a look, I'm sure I could identify what this is if I have a look" he didn't know that, but he was desperate.

The Officer beckoned the man in the suit over and spoke with him just out of the earshot of the crowd, using his hand to cover his mouth so any budding lip readers couldn't interpret what he was saying. The man in the suit walked over, he beckoned David over the cordon who obliged by doing an impression of a hurdler after one too many drinks. As he regained his composure he approached the man who held out a clear plastic exhibit back. David stared at the contents….as his pupils adjusted and his brain finally identified what his eyes were seeing, he knew his life would never be the same again.

JPL, California - "Debra, there's somebody on the phone asking for the senior person." The phraseology that might have offended her until recently, she reached out as Jess passed her the office phone.

"Hello, my name is Debra Johnson, how can I help?" She was curt but polite.

"My name is Professor David Harris from Princeton University. I'm currently in Central Park next to something that seems to have crashed. I think I know what it is....." he stopped himself, almost as if he doubted himself.

"Go on" beckoned Debra.

"I've just seen a fragment pulled from the wreckage. There's a pattern with lines coming out from the centre on it, it looks like it's a fragment of a disk-shaped object. It's yellow......or gold in colour...."

'Voyager' Debra mouthed before David needed to say it himself.

"Who else knows about this?"

"I've not told anybody what my thoughts are yet but they're gonna start asking me questions soon."

"David, I need you to listen to me, this is a matter of National security. I need you to secure that object and ask the officers to secure the scene. I am going to make some phone calls, we need to examine this thoroughly. David, this is now classified information, do you understand? Nobody is to know about your theory." Debra had no idea whether she had the authority to make it classified but she was taking no chances. Was this really Voyager? Which spacecraft was it?

"Debra.....you're gonna want to see this!!" The rest of the team was still oblivious to the finding. Debra put the phone down and walked back towards the TV screen, still showing breaking news. This was a cutover from a Japanese news channel reporting an object having crashed into Yoyogi Park in the centre of Tokyo. Her brain could barely process what she was watching as she saw fire engines dowsing a smouldering wreck in a small crater. It looked like it was made of metal.

"Another asteroid has hit the earth on this remarkable day" announced an excited news anchor. "Japanese authorities are not commenting but this one looks very similar to the asteroid in Central Park."

"Can we try and get a close shot of that?" asked Debra. They checked across news channels until they got a close-up from a helicopter that revealed what she feared. It was not made of rock, it was twisted charred metal.

"Ok listen up, that phone call was from a professor at the scene in Central Park" Debra said as she turned back towards the group. "He has confirmed it was a metal object and I think we've identified it" The fear etched on her face was palpable, the group were silent, every single eye transfixed on her. She gulped, "We think the object in Central Park is one of the two Voyager spacecraft".

Like a chorus, there was a gasp from the team, nobody spoke. "The professor has identified what looks to be part of one of the gold discs, it's just the bottom left corner and shows clearly the pulsar map. It has crossed my mind that it may be an elaborate hoax but this object has now been secured and will be sent to us for examination, together with the wreckage albeit that may take a day or two to arrive."

Still no response from the team. "Now we've got the crash in Tokyo, I can't help but think that's the other Voyager craft. It goes without saying the President is now being made aware and we will be seeking cooperation from the Japanese authorities to secure and return the object to us for examination. I'm guessing we will start to see the telemetry over the coming 24 hours change markedly if this is the two craft, we are just waiting for the signals to catch up."

All of a sudden the alarm on the Voyager 1 tracker sounded and showed a new location, shortly later the same happened for Voyager 2. Voyager 1's distance dropped in an instant.....from around 15 billion miles to 3,000. Roughly the distance from Pasadena to New York. Voyager 2's distance dropped from billions of miles, down to around 5,500, roughly the distance from Pasadena to Tokyo. "I think we got our answer" acknowledged Debra. "Our radio signals are no longer taking 24 hours to reach them, it's happening in minutes."

The White House, Washington DC: The President was in the Oval Office, sat behind the giant 'Resolute Desk', an imposing six-foot-long solid oak desk made using the timber from the old British Expedition Ship, HMS Resolute. A gift from Queen Victoria to President Rutherford B. Hayes in the late 19th century, it was one of many artefacts within the President's Office which fascinated him. The President was catching up on early afternoon security briefings from the CIA and watching the news in the background.

"Mr President, the NASA administrator is on the line."

"I'll take it" responded President Williams, an eye still on the news broadcast showing the scenes in Tokyo and New York. "Bill, what is it with these asteroids?" The President didn't seem too perturbed by what was unfolding in front of him, he assumed it was a coincidence.

President Williams was mid-way through his first term in office. A career politician, his rise to the top had been as unexpected as it had been rapid. Outwardly confident, inwardly he suffered from imposter syndrome and was full of self-doubt.

"It's complicated Mr President" responded the administrator. "Firstly, they're not asteroids, they're not made of rock, they're both metal"

"What? Metal? Wait, are you saying it's the Russians?"

"No, sir….."

"The Chinese?"

"They've not come from earth, sir. I need to explain what's been happening"

"Go ahead Bill, you have my undivided attention."

"Thank you, sir, for the last few days we have been tracking some anomalistic readings from the two Voyager spacecraft, currently speeding through interstellar space. It started with Voyager 1 and at first, we thought they were just glitches in the software. It then happened to Voyager 2 which, as I'm sure you know, is nowhere near Voyager 1 and operates completely independently from it. Then came the biggest surprise of all, Voyager one switched its own camera on, a camera we switched off for good over 30 years ago. The camera shouldn't work but it did and took a number of pictures, the last of which has stunned us all."

"Why is this the first I'm hearing of this Bill?" The President was furious as much as he was confused.

"It's all happened very quickly sir, I have fed it up the line through your office but there's been no time for a full briefing. The last picture sir, you need to see it, is there a secure email address I can send it to?"

"Listen let's video call" suggested the president, "and you can share the picture with me that way" The president transferred the phone back to his secretary who set up the video conference in an instant, the president opened his laptop and plugged it in, transferring from his small laptop screen to a large screen on the wall. "Hey Bill, always better to see who I am talking to, let's have a look at this picture." The president was still relatively upbeat, not really sure what was coming next.

Bill Miller had been the NASA administrator for four years and had spoken with the President several times whilst in post. The two men got on well which was aided by the President's fascination with all things space.

"Ok sir, I'm going to put it up now, let me know when you can see it"

"Will do Bill, it's just coming on now...........Holly shit!!"

"Sir, we believe this is the first contact with extraterrestrial life."

"What?!……"

"Within just over 24 hours of that picture being taken, we believe Voyager One has travelled 15 billion miles and crashed into Central Park. Voyager Two has now landed in Yoyogi Park in Tokyo having also travelled billions of miles in a relatively short period. Both wreckages have now been secured and are on their way to the Jet Propulsion Laboratory in California for examination. We have recovered part of the gold disc from Voyager one and that's on its way too. Looking at all of the facts as we know them, sir, this is not a hoax. We currently have more questions than answers."

There was silence……..

"Ok," the President was absolutely dumbfounded and couldn't muster a meaningful response.

"Sir, as you can imagine we are dealing with this as a national security threat. There is no logical way those two spacecraft could have transversed that distance in that amount of time without help. We can't discount that whatever helped these two craft to earth, are on earth themselves."

"Bill, are you saying there may be extraterrestrial life on Earth?"

"That's exactly what I am saying, sir."

Yoyogi Park, Tokyo: sirens and red and white lights filled the air as a crane started to lift the smouldering wreckage of what was now known to be Voyager 2. As the crane moved upwards, the trees around Yoyogi Park rustled as if being blown by the wind, however the air was completely still. This was followed by a stark freezing cold gust of air.

In Tokyo and New York, those watching on had no idea they were being watched and studied by a species from far, far away.

8

New York: "Where are we going, David?" Quizzed Lizzie.

"I need to get back to our hotel room so I can get on the laptop. I think those weather movements near Saturn are linked to this somehow, I don't know exactly how, I just think they are. I've got the photos on my laptop and I told Debra from the Jet Propulsion Laboratory that I'd send them to her as soon as I can. That lump of metal has travelled billions of miles in hours, my head can't even comprehend how that's possible but I'm sure the blue lights near Saturn have something to do with it, it's too much of a coincidence."

They walked across Central Park to their hotel and then back into their room. David opened his laptop on the small table by the window, pressed a button and it sprung into life. He clicked through several folders until he found the folder he created a couple of days previously in which he had stored the photos he had taken of what he believed at the time were weather phenomena. Lizzie was in the background unpacking clothes and storing them in a tall dark wooden closet. "Coffee?" She asked. "Huh? Oh, yes please?" Replied a distracted David as he started to attach the photos to emails which he then sent to Debra. "Done!" Proclaimed David as he fired the final email off to Debra. "How about that drink then, I could really sink a beer right now?"

"Thought you'd never ask" replied Lizzie as she picked up her coat by the collar and swung it around her in one swift movement. David snapped his laptop shut and they both made their way towards the door. As David pushed the handle down, his phone sounded. "Hello"

"David it's Debra, can we talk."

"Sure, did you get the pictures?"

"I did and I've just sent you a picture, are you in a position to view it?"

"Yeh, hang on a sec'" David walked back towards his desk and opened his laptop again, as it lit up he went into his emails. At the top was an unopened email from Debra which he clicked on and saw one image attached. "Yeh I've got it Debra" he proclaimed.

"Ok, open it"

"Done......what?"

"Ok David, this is an image from Voyager 1 a couple of nights ago. As I'm sure you know the camera on Voyager 1 has not been operational since 1990. A few nights ago we got some strange readings from the spacecraft, then it turned its camera on. The first picture was just a dark image, nothing too dramatic, this is the second image."

David stared at the image, showing a largely black image, with a white circle in the centre of the screen. It appeared to be an electric blue and wasn't a perfect circle but had what appeared to be bolts of electricity arcing off to the sides.

"Now I've got your pictures David, but they won't be as clear as what you saw with the naked eye. Could this be the same phenomenon you witnessed from your telescope?"

"I guess it could be, similar colouring and the electric bolts look similar too. Is there any way we can get a better image" responded David.

"Once the phenomenon was spotted and NASA had caught up with the social media hype around it, they directed the James Webb Space telescope towards it to capture some images. It's going to take a while until we have those images to hand but they will give us a far clearer picture, certainly the best we can get."

David's mind was racing as he started to wonder what had been happening. Had this unusual phenomenon effectively thrown the spacecraft back to Earth? His wonderment was soon interrupted abruptly by Debra. "David, I'm going to send you another picture. This picture is classified but it probably answers the questions you have going through your mind. David......this picture is highly classified, do you understand?"

"I do" responded David....' but what could it be?' He thought. Surely there's nothing more dramatic than the picture Debra had already sent. As he sat, mind racing, his laptop made a 'ding' sound as the next email arrived from Debra. He clicked on the bold font title, saw the image icon and clicked on it...........

Silence

"David, I'm going to explain what you are looking at," Debra said gently. "That is another picture taken by Voyager 1. This is not the original, we've run several colour filters through to get the coloured image you are now looking at". She paused for a few seconds to let it sink in......she continued. "Our most coherent theory is that it's the first contact with extraterrestrial life. It looks like a creature, an entity of some kind. There doesn't appear to be a craft of any kind and it appears to be existing in open space, in a vacuum effectively, without any protection. The blue bolt you saw may well be how they traverse long distances and they may have used Titan as a useful stop-off on the way to Earth. We don't know how they found us, there is a pulsar map on the part of the gold disc which you recovered, thing is that's designed to map earth from a much further distance, the other theory we are working on is that they have effectively followed the radio signals between us and the two Voyager spacecraft." David's heart sank and he felt his stomach knot up.

"Does this mean........they're amongst us?" Blurted David. Lizzie looked on wondering what had made the colour drain from his face. He was not known to be a particularly excitable person, in fact, he was known for the opposite.

"Are you ok?" Mouthed Lizzie. David hardly acknowledged her, he just raised his flat hand to her. There was no way Lizzie was going to take that as an answer and she wandered over behind him so she had a view of his screen, she looked at the image and was suddenly overcome with emotion as her conscious became aware of what it was. She dramatically slammed her left hand over her mouth then her other hand on top as her eyes became moist with tears. David remained focused on his conversation with Debra.

"We can't discount that they are amongst us, did you see anything unusual aside from the obvious, in Central Park" David thought back, although it was only a short time since his discovery, his mind had distorted his perceptions and it now felt like days ago.

"You know, now you say it, something felt strange. It felt like we were being watched and the one thing that stuck out in my mind was that the trees were rustling despite it being a still day, the temperature also dropped suddenly." David felt a chill down his spine as he imagined how these creatures were watching him from the trees. "They could still be Central Park, what are we going to do?"

"We have made the President aware through the administrator for NASA. This is potentially the human race's first contact with Extra Terrestrial life. We don't actually know they are here and, assuming they are, what their intentions are"

They didn't have to wait long to find out.

New York City and its population of over eight million people consume a monstrous amount of energy in the form of electricity and gas. Since the development of the world's first electricity generation and distribution system in the 1880's by Thomas Edison, New York has continued to expand to a point where nearly 1.5% of all electricity generated in the United States, feeds New York City. There are twenty-four power plants which feed New York and between them generate over 9500 megawatts of electricity, enough to supply 80% of what New York needs. The largest Power Station in New York itself is Ravenswood Power Station, located in Long Island City in the Borough of Queens, built in the 1960s and characterised by its four large red and white striped chimneys. An old-fashioned fossil fuel eater, it uses mainly fuel oil and natural gas. Ravenswood is planned for closure in the near future and conversion to a centre for renewable power but for the time being, it continues to generate electricity in the traditions of America's industrial past.

Ravenswood Power Plant, 20:00 hrs, Wednesday: As the sun dipped below the furthermost red and white chimney, the lights flickered on in the station as it continued to work to power New Yorkers. The night shift was just starting and the energy was high amongst the workforce. They had no idea they were being watched and studied by creatures from another planet, creatures far more sophisticated than humans, creatures with capabilities far beyond our own. The lights shimmered off the East River on a still and calm Autumn night as seagulls darted between the chimneys.

"Another shift down!" proclaimed Doug, he was a thirty-year veteran of the power station and was now counting down his days to retirement. Whilst technically it was the beginning of his shift, nobody had the energy to challenge him.

"God dammit Doug, what next, hours and minutes?" Responded one of his colleagues with a huge grin on his face. His work colleagues were not the only ones Doug routinely bored with his retirement countdown, Jackie his wife of 40 years Jill and his two sons, now in their twenties, also got their fair share. The thing was, none of them really minded. Doug was one of those genuine nice guys, who loved to help people and would sacrifice himself in order to do so. He was a father figure to so many workers at the plant, had helped bring through an entire generation of new employees and, unbeknownst to him, was about to be the recipient of the biggest surprise retirement party ever seen at Ravenswood.

"Did anybody see that thing crash into Central Park earlier? Looked like an asteroid or something." Proclaimed Doug.

"No man, been sleeping for the night shift, an asteroid you say?" Responded Jack, a friend of almost 20 years and another senior worker at the plant.

"Yeh, but rumour is it's Russian, maybe a satellite or something" replied Doug as they both nodded to each other to acknowledge they'd just solved a problem currently defeating NASA's most brilliant brains. Doug opened his locker and put his sandwich box inside, pastrami and slaw tonight, his favourite. He took his heavy-duty industrial boots and slipped them on, mirroring Jack, and then the two old friends walked out of the locker room and into the main corridor, complaining about how the Russians fought dirty as they did so.

CRACK!!!

Both men were suddenly thrown to the floor. It sounded like thunder but from within the building. They looked at each other, wide-eyed, fear dripping from every sinew. They felt a sudden cold and something moving at speed through them as lights flickered. Doug tried to settle himself by touching the wall, he felt it breath. This was huge, an earthquake? But nobody was screaming and the ground didn't move, then...........

Nothing.

The factory fell silent, the lights now dark, the voices that had given life to the giant power station for over half a century not even a whisper. Doug? Well, he never did make his retirement. Before

Doug breathed his final breath, he saw a creature in front of him, black and red in colour, then no more.....over sixty years of life extinguished in a heartbeat.

"What the......" The lights dimmed in David and Lizzie's hotel room as the immediate loss of juice supplied by Ravenswood impacted the City. Traffic lights switched off and shops went dark as the impact rippled across the city. Within five minutes the emergency protocol kicked in, electricity was diverted and increased from other sources and power was restored. In the background, the TV in the room flicked back on and the 24-hour news channel continued broadcasting. They could see the news anchor looking around in bewilderment.

"Casey, we have just had a big power outage here in downtown Manhattan, all of a sudden I could see street lights switching off and buildings going dark." Casey was watching intently from the studio. "Hang on, looks like it's back, must have been a power surge. It's been a surreal day here in New York and for a second I wondered what was next." If only he could fathom the enormity of what had just happened.

The White House, Washington DC: "Mr President, we have had something unusual happen in New York" One of the President's aids had run into the Oval Office as the President continued to struggle to understand the unfolding Voyager landings in Central Park and Tokyo.

"I know Laurence, I've been dealing with this all day" he looked incredulous.

"No, sir you don't understand. The biggest power plant in New York City has gone silent, just like that. No warning, no communication since and nobody has been able to make contact. They've managed to redirect power and use backups from elsewhere so there was only a noticeable impact for less than five minutes but nobody knows what's happened. We are awaiting an update from the emergency services at the scene but I thought you'd want to know"

The President sat back in his chair and rubbed his eyes with the thumb and index finger of his right hand, nudging his spectacles higher up his nose. "Thanks, Laurie" he sounded less impatient as if he realised Laurence was doing exactly what he'd always told him to do, act on his initiative. "As soon as we have any update I need to know."

Long Island City, Queens, New York City: several NYPD cars arrived at the metal gates which marked the entrance to the Ravenswood Generating Station. To the left and right of the electric gate were red brick walls with razor wire on top, this obstacle stretched the length of the perimeter. Looking at the gate, the huge building stretched off to the right and large electric pylons stretched off to the left. The area was characterised by the gentle hum that surrounded the plot, but tonight that characteristic hum wasn't there, it was silent. In fact, the entire site was silent, it was as if it was derelict.

The officers got out of their vehicle and walked up to the closed gate. They had a master key that allowed access in case of emergencies and it took three of them to heave the gate back once the key was in place. They drove the three patrol cars into the car park, stepped out of their vehicles, drew their side arms and made their way towards the steps which led to the main entrance. As they walked up the steps, they saw the door half open, leading to the darkness within. They tentatively opened the door and entered torch first, followed by their sidearms, then themselves. As they walked into the building they each shuddered as darkness gave way to cold, they made their way through the building to where minutes before, there'd been a hustle and bustle of dozens of people commencing their work.

The White House, Washington DC: "Sir, you're going to wanna take this" The President looked across his table at his secretary, in his head, he was thinking 'what now?'. "It's the attorney general sir"

"Evening Bob, what've ya got?"

"Sir, I've just had a call from the FBI about the sudden power loss in New York. Cops have attended the Ravenswood Generating plant which was working within normal parameters immediately before the power loss. There should be around 36 men working there this evening and the power plant is currently at full capacity. Sir, I've just been contacted by the FBI…………" he paused briefly to allow his brain to catch up with his mouth. "I've just been contacted by the FBI……..it's empty sir, nothing is left".

"What do you mean nothing is left?" Beckoned the president

"I mean nothing Mr President. No people, no generators, no gas no oil……nothing, it's all gone".

"You mean no bodies? No nothing?"

"That's correct sir, no hint of anything. The CCTV is web-based so there is a chance we may get something on that, we are checking that now. The agents have reported a sudden temperature drop within the building too, almost independent of the surrounding environment."

"OK, this is concerning but let's not overreact. We have potentially got extraterrestrial beings on our planet for the first time......that we know of. Likely locations at this time are Tokyo and New York, where the two Voyager aircraft are believed to have returned to Earth. Now, we have a power station effectively emptied in a way we couldn't do if we wanted to."

"That's correct sir"

The President went to the main door, opened it, popped his head out and called out to his secretary

"I need to speak to the joint chiefs, Secretary for Homeland Security, NASA administrator, Vice President and my chief of staff in 30 minutes in the cabinet room"

She nodded and picked up the phone to start making arrangements. This was now a potential national emergency and the president didn't have time for niceties.

"Bob, I need to know what those cameras show, if anything. Do the FBI now have control of the site?"

"Yes sir, I'll see to it you have those updates"

The president put the phone down and glanced at the TV again, news was still focused on the crashed voyager spacecraft, they were as yet oblivious to the real story. The President didn't know how long it would be before something leaked out so decided to brief the Prime Minister of Japan so he didn't find out from the press. By now it was the following morning in Japan and they needed to now work together to share any intelligence on what they knew. Over the next thirty minutes, the President methodically talked through everything he knew about events thus far as the Prime Minister of Japan struggled to take it on board. As great allies, it was not difficult to agree about what they would share and his Japanese compatriot had already agreed to return Voyager two to the United States so it could

be examined.

9

The White House, Washington DC, 0100 hrs, Thursday: The president threw the door to the cabinet room open as those waiting inside respectfully took to their feet. The huge brown wooden table was sparsely dressed for this impromptu meeting and the president had permitted for laptops to be on so they could receive updates as they spoke.

"Please, sit. We've got a lot to go through." Said the president as he waved his arms downwards. The president took his seat and looked around the table at some of his most senior officials. "Right folks, I don't know how much you all know so I am going to brief you on what I know. Before I start, it goes without saying this is highly classified information, not to go beyond this room".

As he sat, all eyes fixed on him, even the semi-lit busts on the walls appeared to steer their gaze towards the president. He opened his notepad, still a fan for the pen and paper, and started reading. "This is what I know so far" the president proclaimed. "Over the last few days, the Jet Propulsion Laboratory and NASA have been studying some strange readings on the two Voyager Spacecraft. Both craft were launched back in 1977 and were billions of miles away from Earth. At some point, the cameras on both craft were switched on for the first time in over 30 years and started taking pictures. These had been switched off to preserve power and were no longer considered to be functional, they were effectively redundant, sacrificed to keep the craft going. One of the pictures taken shows what appears to be a blue bolt of electricity coming from Voyager 1 itself. At around the same time, astronomers from Earth began observing a strange blue bolt near Saturn, believed to be coming from Titan, its largest moon. The final picture we saw came again from Voyager 1, it appears to show a creature, looking into the camera. There is no craft and the creature doesn't have eyes in the way we do and it appears to be red and black in colour. As we were digesting those photos there were the two asteroids landing in Central Park in New York and Yoyogi Park in Tokyo, they were not asteroids, they were the two Voyager aircraft, they had travelled Billions of miles in a matter of hours and returned to earth. I can now confirm we have reason to believe they were not alone......."

140

Mouths were wide open, eyes transfixed, audible gasps sounded around the dimly lit cabinet room. "Take it in Gentlemen, this is huge, and it doesn't end there." The only man actually writing at this point was General Carter and this latest announcement even forced him to stop and put his pen down. "Obviously, at this time we can't be absolutely sure what the intentions of these creatures are, or their capabilities, but I think we've just found out. This evening, at the Ravenswood Generating Facility in New York, we've had what we believe is the first contact. You may have seen in the news that there was a short power cut in the city before electricity was restored. The FBI has now confirmed to me that Ravenswood, which at this time should have a few dozen men and women inside it working, is empty. There is no sign of them and no sign of a struggle, the station is also dry, and all of the gas and oil used to generate power is gone. We considered they had been abducted but we managed to recover the CCTV which had been uploaded to the cloud. It was filmed in real time but even so, it happened so quickly we can't slow it down enough to see what happens. I am going to show you on the screen what occurred"

The President nodded at his chief of staff, who dimmed the lights, clicked on the file marked 'RW', opened it and pressed play. The clip showed Doug and his colleague walking along the corridor. As the video was slowed down you could see the lights flicker then large red and black creatures for one frame before everybody disappeared. The chief of staff put the lights back up.

"We are now pretty sure that all those men and women have been killed, potentially consumed by these creatures. We also believe they have taken all the fuel from the generating facility. We have no intelligence on their current location. There you go, that's where we are and that's why you're all now involved, any questions?"

There was stunned silence around the room. The president looked slowly from left to right at each man as they stared back, dumbfounded. "Well I have one" he said, in the absence of any response. "How do we make contact with them? I sure as hell don't fancy going head to head with them until we have had a chance to try and communicate with them first. So gents, any ideas?" Still nothing.

"Mr President, have we checked if there were any frequency changes near Ravenswood when they attacked it? Any changes to radio waves? Any interference with computers or anything that can give us a clue as to how they communicate with each other? Find that out and we have the answer" quizzed the NASA administrator.

General Carter glanced sideways at him and responded "We have electronic warfare specialists I can put onto that, see if there were any unusual surges."

"Thanks, General" replied the President. "In answer to your question Bill, no we haven't managed to ascertain as to whether or how they are communicating. Perhaps you can look at if we picked up anything on satellites or comms with Voyager and work with the General to see if there's any commonality"

"Certainly sir" responded the administrator.

"Mr President, have there been any other signs or indicators these creatures are nearby?" asked General Carter.

"Witnesses at the New York and Tokyo crash sites both reported a rapid drop in air temperature near both Voyagers, unusual given the fact that both craft would have been emitting a substantial amount of heat having burned through the atmosphere. Early enquiries near Ravenswood have indicated a significantly cold environment within the buildings, even ice on some of the walls. Some of the footage from both of the crash sites show rustling trees and lawns near the voyager aircraft, yet there was no breeze"

"So extreme cold and potential signs of movement?" Enquired the NASA Administrator.

"That's correct" responded the president. "Gentlemen, at some point I am going to have to tell the good folk of this country what's been happening, you can imagine how that will go down. I don't want to cause panic across the world if I can avoid it so I need to know more,

144

more about what they are, more about why they're here and more about their capabilities. One more thing, I have asked for both Hubble and James Webb Space Telescopes to be turned towards Saturn. We need to know if more are coming. This could be an extinction event if we don't act now."

"Sir"……..General Carter paused before he continued "Have we considered this may be from closer to home?"

"I'm sorry Mike, you've lost me" responded the President with incredulity.

General Mike Carter was Chairman of the Joint Chiefs of Staff and therefore the most senior military officer in the US Armed Forces. He had been the principal Military advisor to President Williams since he assumed office fourteen months previously and the two men had a healthy respect for one another.

General Carter was a nearly 50-year veteran of the US Armed Forces having joined the US Marine Corps in the 1970's and seeing combat in almost every theatre the States had been active in since. He was a largely calm individual, unflappable when things got serious he was very straight talking and nobody could be under any misgivings about the strength, power and credibility he possessed. The President trusted General Carter and knew that he would get the real picture from him, he didn't do sugar coating, refreshing for a President who was often surrounded by sycophants.

"Well, could it be the Russians or Chinese? The Chinese have been developing artificial intelligence at an alarming rate, could it be that?"

"Mike, nothing is off the table. We need to make contact with both heads of state and ask. The best case scenario is you're right, and we are at war."

"That's the best-case scenario Sir?" Responded General Carter.

"Yes Mike, the worst case scenario is we are under attack from advanced extraterrestrial life and the fate of human existence is under threat."

The room remained silent briefly, broken by the President. "We will meet back here in sixty minutes, I need answers." With that he stood up, pushing his chair away from the massive desk, and left the room. He moved through the corridor and back into the Oval Office, asking for a coffee as he moved, sat down on the couch and collected his thoughts briefly. There is no manual for what to do if aliens attack, he was going to have to make this up as he went along. Was he up to the job? He didn't know, but one way or the other he was about to find out.

10 Downing Street, London, United Kingdom, 08:00 hrs, Thursday: "Prime Minister, the President of the United States is on the line, says it's urgent". The Prime Minister had spent the morning dealing with another drama within his own political party and had little time for a conversation with his closest ally.

In his second term as the British Prime Minister, David Stewart was starting to lose popularity with the general public. Add to that, numerous scandals involving members of his party, and he felt like he was permanently 'fire fighting'. Only an hour earlier he had received a call in his private study within 10 Downing Street from one of his most senior ministers. He had warned the Prime Minister that he had been having an affair with one of his staff and the story was likely to break in the press and social media imminently as a photo had leaked of them kissing. He had offered his resignation but the Prime Minister refused to accept it. He'd already lost his best friend and political ally when they were found to have committed tax fraud and he couldn't afford to lose another good minister. Recognising how this would be interpreted by the public, he had spent the rest of the morning video conferencing with his comm's manager to plan how they could get ahead of the story, or upstream as the comm's manager preferred to call it.

He had just settled back into his large leather office chair to take a breath when the President called. He picked up his cup of fresh Earl Grey tea, blew the top of the cup reassuringly, breathed in the familiar floral scent and beckoned his secretary in. She entered and passed the phone over, he grabbed it, blew the front hairs of his fringe indicating just what kind of morning he was having and spoke with his greatest ally.

"Mr President, how are you?"

"David, not good, I need you to listen carefully to what I'm about to tell you"

The President proceeded to go through what had happened to this point and the theories as to what had caused it. The Prime Minister sat in his chair, staring at the dark wood-panelled walls, mouth open.

"Are there any signs they are anywhere other than the States at the moment?" Asked the PM.

"Yes, the second Voyager spacecraft landed in Tokyo. I have informed the Japanese PM, that nothing further has happened there that we are aware of but we must assume they are there too. Don't forget David, if these creatures are what we think, they have travelled billions of miles in a matter of hours. It won't take much for them, to cross the Atlantic. I am going to inform the rest of Europe's leaders and other allies before I address the American public. It's my view that we are at war, but we don't know who against."

Fukushima Nuclear Power Plant, Fukushima Prefecture, Japan, 17:00 Thursday: Following the great earthquake of 2011, the plant had been disabled due to radiation leaks and damaged reactors. A small workforce was based at or near the plant and they were tasked with the dismantling of the structure over the coming decades, a highly complex and expensive process expected to cost over $150 billion.

Hidetoshi Sumeda was in his early 40s and had been working at the plant for the last seven years. He was charged with the management of water purification from one of the reactors and loved the challenge his job provided on a daily basis.

As the afternoon drew to a close, Hidetoshi was sweltering in his double-layered protective equipment, necessary to protect workers from the dangers of contamination. He had spent the afternoon, as he had many before it, monitoring radiation levels in tanks outside the main reactors and ensuring that they remained within safe levels. Whilst a dangerous choice of career it was highly rewarded and afforded Hidetoshi the lifestyle he craved. With a love of 1980's Japanese Sports cars and an obsession with expensive European watches his choice of career and willingness to accept risk was a necessary byproduct. Hidetoshi's wife of twenty years worked in Tokyo with the Bank of Japan and they lived to the north of the giant city in a small house with a perfectly kept garden.

Hidetoshi moved over to one of the pipes and read off the temperature to his colleague "seventy-three" he said. They moved together to the next pipe across the tarmac, and as they did so they felt a movement in the air, despite there being no breeze. Hidetoshi looked down at the temperature gauge "Huh, this can not be!" He remarked. The pipe was frozen and, as he glanced down at the temperature gauge, the temperature read minus 700 degrees Celsius.

Suddenly............

Nothing.

Nothing was left, everything and everybody had disappeared. The plant had been emptied and left a shimmering ice grave. As for Hidetoshi? Well, he never did get to drive his 80's Japanese Sports cars again.

His Majesties Naval Base, Faslane, Clyde, Scotland, that same day: A Rubis Class French Nuclear submarine, a Virginia Class American Nuclear sub and HMS Vanguard and Victorious, two British nuclear-powered ballistic missile submarines were in port.

"How many sausages can one person eat?" Lance chuckled at David as he ate his sixth sausage of the morning. Lance and Dave were both engineering technicians on board one of the United Kingdom's primary nuclear deterrents. They had known each other for several years and were great friends on and off the boat. Dave had a substantial appetite and a metabolism that most would die for which meant he stayed at around twelve stone regardless of what he ate. "Seriously mate, I bet you'll have a full lunch too" Both men chuckled as they sat at a small table in the mess of HMS Vanguard. "You looking forward to being back out at sea Lance?" Dave spluttered between mouthfuls of Lancashire's finest sausages. "You know what? I am, I just love how we are alone out there, alone with the people I trust the most. Fresh air is overrated" he chuckled. HMS Vanguard was being deployed to the Gulf via Cyprus, a journey both men knew well. "Will we get any time in Cyprus?" Enquired Dave as he moved from sausage demolition onto bacon consumption. "Well, I really hope…….." his retort was interrupted by a sudden movement of the submarine to the port side and a massive drop in temperature, followed by…………

Nothing.

All four nuclear submarines bobbed in the water…..empty. No people, no warheads, no nuclear reactors. Complete silence suddenly fell over the area as it took the three navies time to understand what had happened. Lance and Dave had eaten their very last breakfast.

10 Downing Street, one hour later: "Nothing?!" Screamed the prime minister. He was stood behind his desk, hands gripping the edge, partly through fear and partly through anger.

"Nothing Prime Minister. All four subs, two of ours and one each from France and the US were in port. Nothing is left apart from the hulls. It's like four icy carcasses left for us as a demonstration. But the other thing…." The British Defence Secretary responded.

"Tell me there's nothing else!!" Spluttered the prime minister.

"That's just the point, there is nothing else, nothing at all. They've been stripped of all the nuclear reactors and the nuclear warheads. They're just gone. All four subs are now just empty shells, frozen empty shells. I have asked for any footage and it's being downloaded now, I'll see to it you get it once it's done. I've also asked for radar and sonar readouts, I just can't believe this isn't something or somebody more obvious."

"What do you mean?" Enquired the prime minister.

"I mean the Russians or Chinese. Surely this is them and we are being sidetracked by the American's sci-fi dreams. We can't afford to take our eyes off the ball here. I have the chief of the defence staff scouring hostile nations to see if we can find a more rational explanation."

"Thank you, do that in the background and we maintain our focus, I've got some phone calls to make then a full cabinet meeting in sixty minutes before I address the House of Commons. Thank you" responded the prime minister.

10

Jet Propulsion Laboratory, Pasadena, Friday, 0630 hrs: "How is this so well preserved? I mean, I've checked everything I can without taking it apart completely, it's still pretty much functional," remarked Gus, tweezers in one hand and screwdriver in the other, surgical mask over his mouth and nose.

He was systematically checking through the wreckage of Voyager 1. The Spacecraft was now in sections and this section was now sitting on a huge table in the room, within a sealed clear glass box. It had multiple circles cut out where gloves were inserted and multiple spotlights were shining down on it.

"I literally cannot believe this was billions of miles away literally days ago, look, even parts of the gold disc are still on here" he smiled as he held a fragment of the gold disc in his tweezers before placing it carefully into a small transparent bag. "Do we have any idea when Voyager 2 will arrive back?"

"No, not at all, it's coming via the Air Force so I'd imagine it's any time now" responded Jess.

Both were tasked with taking apart and documenting the two spacecraft together with several others. It was a slow and painstaking process which would take days of working all hours. So far they had found no explanation as to how these two craft had managed to find themselves back on earth. Each tiny piece of metal needed to be swabbed for DNA and then placed into two bags, one for the material, and one for the DNA.

Jess stood up from her stool and made her way to the large window overlooking the California desert beyond. She had an uneasy feeling, like something bad was happening. She knew little of the facts but felt a need to go home, to her parents, to be with them. As she stood looking out at the birds and animals outside, the TV news stream in the background suddenly changed with a yellow ticker across the bottom announcing 'President to address the nation at 11:00 EST'.

"Can somebody turn that up?" asked Gus. A series of blank faces and aimless shuffling made it clear nobody knew where the remote control for the TV was so Jess made her way to the TV to do so manually.

The reporter was commenting on possible reasons for the message with the conclusion being that it was related to the recent terrorist attack on Ravenswood Power Station. This was a theory peddled by a number of news outlets and it suited the government to allow that narrative to pervade......until now. Little attention was given by those working on the spacecraft as they continued to methodically take apart Voyager 1.

The White House, Washington DC, 1030 hrs: "Can I get a glass of water for the President please?" one of the White House comm's officers shouted as she fixed the tiny black microphone to the President's lapel. "We are going live in thirty minutes and we can't have his voice going dry on us."

The President read back through his speech and made small corrections with his black pen before handing it to his secretary for it to be re-typed. In the corner of the Oval Office, the first lady stood looking across at him behind his desk, arms folded. Around the president was a flurry of activity, everyone aware this was likely to be the most important presidential speech in their lifetime.

"Ok sir, what you are going to say will be hard for the public to take in, so you must be clear, no ambiguity. We have been scouring international news outlets and social media and, apart from the usual conspiracy theorists, nobody has made any links yet and we've managed to keep a lot of this under wraps." As his Press Secretary said this she smiled at the irony that the foil hat-wearing conspiracy theorists had finally got something right 'I guess a stopped clock has the correct time twice a day' she reflected.

A young suited man entered the Oval Office, the smell of freshly roasted coffee filling the air as he carried with him a mug of coffee for the First Lady, he placed it on a coaster on the table in the corner where she had taken up residency. An army of helpers continued to preen the president and his surroundings.

"Before we go live I'd like ten minutes to myself please." The president said gently, an almost calm aura had swept through him, "Just myself and the First Lady please." Affirmative nods passed through the throng of people and they increased the intensity of their work to ensure they were finished with plenty of time to spare. At 10:50 they started to filter out of the office, leaving just the president and First Lady. He stood up and walked over to the couch and beckoned the First Lady to sit next to him.

President Williams was in his first term and was finding the responsibility of being the leader of the free world a challenge. His party weren't in control of both houses so taking forward his legislative agenda was a struggle. Public opinion was also challenging, he was seen as a nice guy, but not a strong and commanding leader. Sherri was his wife and his rock, her belief in him never wavered and they were a true team. College sweethearts, Sherri had paused her career as a successful attorney to focus on the responsibilities of First Lady, something she took very seriously. Proud parents to two little girls, they doted on them and tried to normalise their lives as best as possible, not easy given their slightly unusual home.

"Sherri, honey, I need you to listen to me. As I give this speech this morning I want you to go with the kids. Marine one is fuelled up and on the lawn waiting to take you to a bunker in the Rockies, I need you all to be safe. I think this is going to get bad…..real bad. We don't even know what these things are capable of yet but I do know one thing, they seem to be attracted to big cities and the military, so I need to get you away from both. I will stay here and lead the fight."

As he was saying these words Sherri was just smiling at him, shaking her head.

"Honey, I'm serious, you need to go"

"No, we are going nowhere. This building is our home and you are my husband. When we got married I agreed for better or worse and that's what I'm gonna do. I will support you and will never leave your side."

The President looked deep into her big brown eyes like he was gazing into the pool of her soul beyond. He realised right there and then that there was no way she would go. With his eyes welling up, he smiled back at her "You are truly my rock, very well.......and thank you"

The First Lady smiled back and stood up, wiped a tear from her eye and said sternly "Right Mr President, you've got a nation to address"

With that, the President stood up, straightened his dark blue jacket and yellow tie, and made his way over to his desk. The doors opened and the wave of people poured back into the Oval Office.

"OK, we are live in two minutes" barked the President's excitable comm's assistant to the room. "Sir, I'll be behind the camera and will count you in". He nodded, shuffled his paper and cleared his throat.

"Five, four, three………."

"My fellow Americans. I am speaking to you today to tell you, that we have been in contact with beings from another world, extra-terrestrial creatures. I will not dress this up, it would appear that their intentions towards us may be aggressive. I can now confirm there are a number of incidents around the world that we have connected and have reason to believe were the work of these creatures. In New York, Japan and the United Kingdom, there have been a number of attacks resulting in the sad and untimely deaths of human beings and I offer my deepest condolences to all those affected. I have been in contact, through the United Nations, NATO and other alliances across the world, with other world leaders. We have pledged to work together to better understand what has happened and how we can resolve this. Using our collective minds and resources, I am confident we can return to normality soon. Before that happens I must ask of you several things. First, ensure your mobile phones remain charged and switched on, any information of note will go out via the emergency broadcasting system and be automatically pushed out to all mobile devices. Second, please follow without question any direction given to you from the Military or law enforcement agencies, it may just save your life. Third and finally, please don't panic. This has been relatively well contained for several days as you can see from the fact it hasn't been reported. That being the case there is no need to make any significant changes to your routines at this time. I will ensure I come back in front of you again when I have more information to update you. Finally, it is my solemn duty to inform you that, as of now, this country is at war and we will release more details about what that means to you shortly.......Thank you and god bless America".

Jet Propulsion Laboratory, Pasadena: the entire room was captivated by the president's speech being broadcast live on the large screen.

"Well, I think you will agree with me, that was a speech none of us expected" responded the newscaster, open-mouthed and clearly in shock. "We have been sent further details from the government which I am now permitted to share" She cleared her throat as if announcing to a packed room. "It is believed the two crashes in Central Park and Tokyo were the two Voyager Space Craft launched from Earth in 1977, its further believed that the beings brought them back to the planet, travelling billions of miles in a matter of hours, these crafts are now being examined at the Jet Propulsion Laboratory for clues as to what happened"

Gus threw his hand up for a high five, a smile spread across his face........he was ignored and sheepishly put it back down again after a few seconds.

"The three incidents that are being investigated were Ravenswood Generating Plant in New York, Fukushima Nuclear Power-plant in Japan and the Faslane military facility in Scotland, a Royal Navy base which houses nuclear submarines. We understand there are no survivors." The newscaster's voice was almost a whisper as she spoke, hardly believing what she was reading. She continued "Before each incident, there was a sudden and significant drop in air temperature, capable of freezing anything in its path. The incidents lasted only a few seconds, so fast modern recording equipment struggles to capture it. Black and red creatures were seen very briefly at each of the three sites, the same black and red creature that was seen staring down the lens of Voyager 1 as it sped through interstellar space. The creatures are not visible to the naked eye aside from these brief revelations. Armed forces from across the world have been moved to the highest alert levels and will respond collectively to any threats. The United States Government have declared a national emergency". She took a sip of water, refocused on the camera and whispered, "Well folks, this could be the first true world war, we'll be back after these words from our advertisers".

There was silence in the room. Gus looked around at the mangled wreckage of Voyager 1 as the rest of the room took in the enormity of what they had just heard. "Well, I guess we'd better get on with this then" he quipped, renewed intent in his voice. He moved back over to the table as the rest of the room continued to watch. Gus seemed far more capable of accepting the announcement as he had suspected something significant was afoot already, ever since the pictures from the Voyagers, the changes in the path of the two craft.

All of this cushioned his consciousness from the announcement. "Come on, we need to do our job!" He coaxed. The rest of the room remained in a trance briefly, then made their way back to their original tasks.

The Whitehouse: "Well done Sir, very commanding performance" The President looked up from his papers, unable to afford a smile.

"Thanks for your help, that was tough" he responded, then got to his feet and accepted a glass of fresh water from his secretary who had just entered the room. He took a grateful sip, removed the handkerchief from his left-hand breast pocket and gently dabbed his forehead. Sherri was back in the corner of the room, smiling gently at the President, he nodded back in acknowledgement.

As the President had given his speech to the American people, similar updates were being coordinated by other world leaders, all giving their citizens similar information. Military leaders began briefing senior military Officers as plans were written to defend key national infrastructure sites. What were they protecting them against? Nobody really knew. Could they mount a defence? Nobody knew, but nations felt they needed to do something. Power plants, military bases, and government buildings, all received a military focus relative to the nation's military resilience. In several nations, war was declared, together with warnings of military mobilisation. The largest military powers mobilised millions of reserves in an instant with the USA, China, India and Russia mobilising over four million reserves collectively alone. This was a threat to human existence and world leaders knew it. Nations that were natural enemies started to talk, sometimes for the first time in years and freely shared information.

The Voyagers, as they had become known by popular media very quickly, had grabbed the attention of the human race, and it was about to get worse.

11

Military bases across the world snapped into action. Live ammunition was removed from crates and countries started to remove equipment stored in case of war. This was the worst-case scenario, the existence of the human race was in jeopardy, and time was of the essence.

Spring Valley, California, United States, Saturday 08:00 hrs: "Chad, call me when you can!!" Marie shouted as Chad lifted his person-sized sports bag over his left shoulder. Chad and Marie Phillips were in their mid-twenties and had met whilst Chad was in training with the US Marine Corps. A few years down the line Marie was used to waving him goodbye as he went off with his friends to far-flung places across the world. This felt different though, he was going to war. Chad was on automatic pilot though and didn't notice the trepidation in her voice.

"Sure Marie, I'll send you a message or something as soon as I can." He appeared mildly irritated but was in fact just trying to remember the details given to him over the phone by his Sgt an hour earlier. He was to report to Camp Pendleton, 38 miles outside San Diego before making the 82-mile journey north to Los Angeles where they would form part of the defence force around the city. He placed his bag into the trunk of his yellow Camaro and walked back to Marie who had waited patiently in the doorway.

"Look after yourself honey, it looks bad out there"

"It was bad in Afghanistan but I'm here ain't I?" His voice softened "Seriously, don't worry, I'll be back before you know it" his confidence betrayed his true feelings. He had seen the presidential address and felt sickness in his stomach as he watched. Fighting humans is one thing, fighting the unknown?......well, that's another. He hugged Marie and she held him tight as he kissed the top of her head.

"I love you...." She whispered under her breath as she watched him climb into his car. She hoped those wouldn't be the last words she said to him.

Richmond, North Yorkshire, United Kingdom: the mist hugged the luscious green valley like a plumped pillow on a green carpet. James was keen to rent a cottage in the countryside once his posting to

Catterick, home of the largest British Army Garrison in the world, had been confirmed and he really had settled into country life. As he watched the tiny birds darting between trees in his garden, his silent musings were interrupted by Chloe, his two-year-old springer spaniel. "Hey Chlo, I haven't forgotten girl, don't worry." His wife, Sarah, smiled at him as he pulled his wax jacket on over his army shirt and took Chloe out for her morning walk.

Major James Tannick had been an officer in the British Army for a decade and a half and was very much a veteran of active service. A proud Company Commander of the Royal Yorkshire Regiment, he had been told his company would be deploying to Manchester where they would form part of the protective force defending the city. James spent his time looking after and leading others so very rarely worried about himself. This was different though, he didn't know what he was up against, or if it could be defeated.

Around the world, similar stories played out as people said goodbye to their families whilst they went to fight something they didn't know about and certainly didn't understand. Most countries prioritised large cities and population centres together with national infrastructure sights such as transport hubs, power stations and military sites. The world was truly at war, perhaps for the first time and were singularly united against their foe.

The White House: "There have been sightings in Europe, Asia and Australia in the last few hours but no new attacks. We have no footage showing them move, even when we slow the footage down the best we get is a red-and-black blur. They are there and then they're not. From what we can tell there are around 36 of them split into three different groups. We are guessing all came down with the two Voyagers and we have yet to establish if they are communicating with each other. We now have battle groups protecting all major cities across the US together with separate forces protecting power stations and other national infrastructure sites. We are sharing information and intelligence, not just with our allies, but with previously hostile states. Sir, if we had only known what Chinese and Russian capabilities were before this......well it would have changed things." The defence secretary thought the president would want to know about his findings on previous enemies.

"It's all changed" snapped the President as he walked across the Oval Office. "These are not our enemies any more they are our allies. We cannot afford to think like that any more, the world has changed, do we understand?" There were tentative nods around the room.

"Sir, we are currently at DEFCON 3, do you plan on changing that?" Quizzed the Defence secretary.

"Yes, set DEFCON 2, we can't afford to delay. We need to be ready to act once we understand the quickest way to destroy these creatures. This is the greatest existential threat to humankind, nothing is off the table." The Secretary of State nodded and left the room to ensure arrangements were made.

Across military bases in Russia, tactical nuclear weapons were prepared to be used in anger. Tactical, as opposed to strategic nuclear weapons, tend to have much smaller explosive yields. This means they are ideal to use on the battlefield where a strategic nuke would cause far too much collateral damage. It is often said that a tactical nuclear weapon is designed to win the battle and a strategic nuke is designed to win the war.

Catterick Garrison, North Yorkshire, UK: "Right lads listen in. We are being deployed to Carrington Power Station as part of the Manchester battle group. We are the spearhead battalion and will be joined by the core elements of the 15th Armoured Brigade. Also joining us will be elements of the United States Air Force to provide air cover as the Royal Air Force is focused on the midlands and south of the country. I know you will be keen to understand our enemy but.......to be honest, we don't know much at the moment. What we do know is they move too fast to see and do not leave anything behind. We have no idea how they kill but we do know that when they move, the temperature in their immediate vicinity drops, markedly. The government has prioritised national infrastructure sites and large population centres, hence we are going to a power station just outside Manchester. Finally....." Lt Col

Greaves, Commanding Officer of the third Battalion of the Royal Yorkshire Regiment, paused for a moment, looking out over his senior officers, sat open-mouthed in front of him. They were all seasoned veterans but this was beyond even their experience. "Ahem.......finally, make sure yours and your officers and soldiers' wills are up to date, we need to prepare for the worst......that is all" With that, the senior officers all stood up and made their way through the main door of the briefing room. All were clutching their notepads, ready to brief their officers and soldiers before they left and made their way West towards Manchester. James was running through in his head what he would tell them but, to be honest, he concluded there wasn't much to tell. There had only been a small number of attacks up to this point so he still found it hard to believe the threat was as high as it was being sold.

The Whitehouse, Washington DC: "Sir, we've had contact from the President of France, there's been another attack, south of Lyon. Casualties around 3,000, the location was a nuclear power plant."

The president was in the Oval Office with two of his generals for an update briefing. The smell of freshly ground coffee filled the air as the three men discussed options and contingency moving forward. The interruption from the intelligence corp Colonel, Wesley Miller, was not expected but necessary to help them continue to adapt their plan.

"Thank you, Colonel, any more details?" Enquired the President.

"No sir, very similar to other attacks, no survivors and no trace of anything remaining"

"Thank you, Colonel"

"You're welcome Mr President" and with that, he left the two generals and the President in the Oval Office.

"Ok gentlemen, that's another attack and thousands more dead. A power station again, that's obviously a target. We need to plot every power station in this country and every major city with details of the military units being used to defend them......." The President was trying to take stock of where everyone was.

"Sir!!" The colonel rushed into the Oval Office again, flustered.

"Colonel, I know, I don't need any further information!" The president was a little irritated as he stood leaning against the main desk, arms spread wide as he looked at a map.

"Sir, there's been another attack...."

The president looked up from the desk. His pupils dilated slightly as he felt his stomach churn with anxiety and his fight or flight reflexes kicked in. "Where?" He asked gently.

"Chicago sir, Braidwood, the nuclear power plant.....but." The Colonel coughed, there was clearly more to this than just that. "Sir, we've lost contact with the US Army 7th Division. They were sent there to defend that part of Chicago and the power plant.......and sir"

"What….." the president swallowed back as he asked, not wanting to hear the answer. "And what, Colonel" he demanded.

"Sir, as soon as we lost contact with the 7th Division we sent fast jets overhead to gather intelligence, the division was no longer there, no trace of them at all, it's as if they'd never been there but even worse, Southland, all of south Chicago is abandoned, completely empty."

"What do you mean empty?"

"I mean empty Mr President, there's no trace of anybody or anything. They've flattened everything, not so much as a dog in a yard remains, houses flattened."

"Colonel, that's 2.5 million people, they can't have just gone!!" The president reacted angrily, thumping the desk, completely unable to take in the enormity of what he was being told. "Send in a search team to get a detailed look at what's happened, maybe the fast jets were mistaken, I also want satellite footage soonest, please. I can't believe they're simply gone."

The president felt himself shaking as adrenaline coursed through his veins and he sat down so others couldn't see it. He grabbed a glass of water from the far side of his desk as he tried to combat the symptoms of shock, forcing it down his throat contrary to his instinct. The two Generals stood next to the desk, staring at each other, pale and clammy as they fought their body's instinct to close down. They looked across at the colonel as the president once more fixed his gaze.

"It goes without saying this is to stay in this room for now, I need more information as soon as possible. I know it's early evening and getting dark so I'm not expecting much from the satellites at the moment but can we get Police helicopters to join the Air Force with thermal imaging over the top to check for heat sources please?" His brain had kicked back in, almost like sitting down and drinking some water had been the hard reset he needed.

"Yes sir, I'll get to it right away" The Colonel left the office, closing the great double wooden doors gently behind him. The president leaned back in his chair looking at the ceiling as he let out a long breath. The Generals stood in silence, watching him and not knowing how to respond.

It was the single greatest loss of human life in one day in the history of human existence. If the number of people the president feared dead was accurate, it exceeded all of the worst military and natural disasters in history by a huge margin. On top of this, the United States had lost an entire Military Division without so much as a whimper. If they were to prevent the end of mankind, an extinction-level event, they were going to have to rethink how they would fight back.

12

Jet Propulsion Laboratory, Sunday 08:00 hrs: "Have any of you managed to sleep in the last 24 hours?"

Debra, fresh from a first full night's sleep in a week, was conducting a morning briefing session in the main lab with every member of the team working on the two Voyager spacecraft. Keen to look after everybody, including herself, whilst ensuring a quick and thorough job was done she checked with each and every person, one by one, how much rest they'd had of late. "I understand why you all want to work night and day, but we must do a thorough and professional job and I don't think we can do that when we are all shattered. Jess, can you put a rota together which ensures everybody has a rest period, please? Now, things have been moving on through the night so I'm going to brief you as to where we are. Before I do, I need an update on what you've found so far."

"Nothing Debra, it's as if they've just been transported here, like in Star Trek. There are marks and burns consistent with them speeding through space but nothing more than that, they are in phenomenal condition. We are now bagging up every outer-facing piece of material the creatures could have come into contact with so we can send them off for forensic examination as a priority, then we will bag up the remaining parts and subject them to the same forensic scrutiny. It's going to take a while though, several more days until we have finished the outside." Gus was one of the team that had worked pretty much non-stop since the first issues with Voyager 1 had become clear. He certainly needed to heed Debra's advice but now had nobody to go home to as he'd sent his husband and child away to his parent's house deep in the Californian Desert. A remote community, they had assessed that it was the best decision for their son.

"Thanks, Gus. Can we send what we have separated to the lab now, the forensic scientists are keen to build a DNA profile of the creatures. We can then get the rest off in the next few days." Debra span her gaze away from the metal hulk of the spacecraft and towards her team. "Right, there have been more attacks overnight, including here in the States. The government are tight-lipped as to casualty numbers but social media speculation is rife and if it's anywhere near accurate......well put it this way, the numbers are spectacular. As you all know, we've had press massed outside here for the last few days. Be really careful what you say to them, it's very easy to misinterpret. Point them towards the NASA press office for the official line. Ok, I won't keep you any longer." With that, she shuffled herself off the table she had perched herself on and walked over to the coffee pot.

"Hey Jess," she said as she poured the lukewarm coffee into her mug. "You ok?"

Jess had wandered over to speak to Debra, concerned that her family may be in danger.

"Debra, you talked about numbers and that they may be spectacular, what did you mean by that? I've been trying to get hold of my family, they've been staying in Chicago visiting relatives for a few days but there's no answer and now their phone line is dead."

"Honestly Jess, I don't know and I really don't want to speculate. If you listen to social media we are probably dead and we know that's not true. Just try and concentrate on your job and don't worry about it. We don't know for sure that anything has happened in Chicago and even if it has what the effect has been. We also don't know the impact on mobile communication in any affected area so even if it has, not being able to contact them isn't necessarily something to worry about" she smiled, a smile that hid more knowledge than she could reveal. Jess smiled back and wandered back to her workstation.

The White House, Washington DC: "Ok Colonel, we'll start with you." The President and his cabinet, together with several senior military commanders, were packed into the Cabinet Room. The smell of fresh coffee and sweet pastries filled the air and the table was decorated with paper maps with marker pen scrawls over them, laptops and mobile phones. The president was eating a Danish pastry as it was the first opportunity he had to eat having worked through the night.

"Sir, I'll go through nation by nation. We are sharing through the intelligence network and, as I understand it, this is the same picture the rest of the countries have." The president nodded. "I'll start here in the US." He drew breath "The first losses were in Ravenswood New York City, with around 3000 people now confirmed dead. Chicago, around two point five million killed yesterday together with a full U.S. Army Division of around fifteen thousand military personnel.....and sir....." he looked up.

"Go on Colonel, what is it?"

"We've now lost contact with the 22nd Division." The president looked across at one of the Generals.

"Where were they?" The President enquired.

"Texas, sir" responded one of the Generals.

"They were based near the South Texas Nuclear Generating Station. There were fifteen thousand personnel. We can't get in touch with the station, the military personnel or anybody from the local town of Bay City. In total, that's around eighteen thousand people in Bay City, fifteen thousand troops and around two and a half thousand at the power station. But sir, it's worse than that….." he opened his laptop and synched it with the screen at the far end of the room. As he cycled through the security screens the President took a sip of water in anticipation. The room was completely silent.

Click…..

"Sir, these are satellite images of Houston, Texas, at 0900 this morning….."

Click…..

"These are satellite images from 1045……"

There were gasps around the room, the pictures showed an abandoned city.

"We've sent aircraft over and nothing sir, nobody is seen. Again, we'll send some teams in to look for survivors but initial indications are there are none. Around two point five million people were living there until this morning sir."

"Right......well." The president scratched his chin, trying to gather his thoughts. "Well, let's just take five minutes please." The president stood up and wandered back to the Oval Office, beckoning for his chief of staff as he left the cabinet room. The remainder of the cabinet sat, in silence, mouths open.

"What am I gonna do?" Asked the president in desperation as he closed the double doors of the Oval Office behind them both.

"Sir, this is going to get worse before it gets better. They've caught us by surprise, we need to get back on the front foot. You need to lead us there Mr President, lead us back from this."

"What will I tell the American people?" Spluttered the President in desperation.

"Well, I don't think now is the time to say any more. Yes, there is serious danger out there, but what are you going to tell them to do? We don't know, all it will do is create panic. I'll talk to the comm's office and pen some 'if asked' lines should rumours start hitting the media. Something like 'we are aware of various rumours concerning casualties, please follow government social media for official announcements', bland but hopefully will put a stop to some of the rumours. In the meantime, we need to finish this intel briefing sir."

"Ok, thanks, Joe. I needed that, let's get back in there." The president managed to muster a smile as they both turned and headed back into the cabinet office.

Joseph (Joe) Davis, was a long-term friend and ally of the President and the only choice when it came to appointing a chief of staff at the beginning of his term. The president knew he could trust Joe in all circumstances and their wives were also firm friends and they had, before the President's election, socialised frequently together.

"OK Colonel, what else have you got?" He had steadied himself again.

"Well sir, it's not good. There have been 27 attacks across China at last count, with casualties potentially in the tens of millions. Key power-generating sites and nearby cities have been hit in a similar way to here but of course, the Chinese don't have the ability to assess the damage in the way we have so I wouldn't like to bet my house on any figures. Again 'click' if you look at this footage from a satellite over Datang Tuoketuo power station, you can see it's been obliterated, 'click' this slide shows the Shanghai Caojing Power Station this morning, again nothing remains. Even worse, there is no sign of life in the entire southern part of Shanghai. The Chinese have confirmed the attacks but not losses."

"Ok, but Shanghai alone could be tens of millions...."

"Yes sir. France is reporting losses in Lyon, Germany in Frankfurt and the East of Berlin, and the UK in Leeds and Birmingham and this is just the last 24 hours. If you add the losses up, we are talking tens if not hundreds of millions and dozens of power plants completely destroyed. Australia, Malaysia, India, Pakistan, Canada and Brazil have all reported losses too. We will have a more in-depth report on what has happened across the world when we get more detail but, as you can imagine, the intelligence community is finding it hard to stay on track with this. One more thing sir….."

"Go on Colonel" the president beckoned as he looked up from his leather-bound notebook.

"The Russians have warned us that, should they manage to corner any voyagers, they would use tactical nuclear weapons to destroy them. You can expect a formal notification from the Russian President soon sir."

"Thank you, Colonel, you may leave unless anybody else has any questions of you?" The president scanned the room but there were no indications so the Colonel left. "Ok, General Carter, where are we with ensuring every major power plant and population centre has military cover?"

"Sir, we are nearly there, I estimate we will have every objective met within the next twelve hours. We are also assisting the Germans, Japanese and the United Kingdom with their defence at this time. Sir, I do have a question and it's a little sensitive"

"Go on General"

"B61's sir, do I have permission to put them on high alert readiness, the Russians already have as you've just heard?"

"Tactical nuclear weapons General?"

"We are facing the biggest ever threat to humanity, if there's even the slightest chance they will work, we need to take it."

The President took a deep breath in through his nose, eyes fixed on General Carter, the most senior Officer in the US Armed Forces. The room was silent, transfixed on the two men.

"General, I can confirm 'cocked pistol'……….ladies and gents, the United States is at Defcon 1"

Defcon 1, or cocked pistol as it's also known, has never been officially declared since its creation in the 1950's. The president's cabinet seemed at once surprised and then accepting, understanding that it could be the only way to save millions of lives. The President had acted decisively.

"I don't have to tell you this is not something we will announce to the public but I know they would expect me, their president, to take all measures necessary to safeguard our nation."

Jet Propulsion Laboratory, California: "Jennifer, I'm hearing some really worrying rumours about the level of casualties, have you heard anything officially?" Quizzed Debra.

Debra and Jennifer were sat opposite each other in one of the conference rooms. It was quiet in there and they both happened to walk in at the same time unplanned, attempting to get away from the main throng of activity.

"No, it's pretty much silence out there, the administrator is chairing almost hourly meetings but he's mainly taking information in, he's not updating us at this stage. I've been hearing the same as you though, to be honest I'm not taking any chances, my family are currently packing up and heading for Montana. The family has a ranch there and it's in the middle of nowhere, I can't see the Voyagers finding enough to interest them there."

"I don't blame you Jen, get them as far from built-up areas as you can."

"What about you Debra, where are your family, are they ok?"

"They're already remote so should be fine for now hopefully. Jen, do you feel we are responsible for this"

"Wow! Where did that come from?" Jennifer sat back on her chair as Debra balanced her forehead on her open hand.

"Well, when I say we, I guess I really mean me. I was part of the team that started the Voyager adventure, surely if it wasn't for us this would never have happened?"

"Ha, Debra, of course, it would. It may not have been now, or even our lifetime, but it was always destined to happen. Look at us, we've been reaching out into outer space for decades, sending radio signals, probes and spacecraft. Trying to make contact with species from another world. How naive were we? What made us think it would end well? Naivety or arrogance, two of humans' worst traits combined." She looked up at the ceiling as she spoke.

"I wonder if we hold the answers? Nobody has spent more time staring out into deep space than us, if only I could clear my head and think this through. We've had some of the greatest minds in the space community working on this since it happened, nothing. Are we missing something obvious?"

"Maybe you're too close Debs, maybe you lose perspective with proximity"

"Yeh maybe" responded Debra, "kinda gets you thinking doesn't it?"

The White House, Washington DC: "Sir, I can confirm the B61's are now prepared and loaded onto US F18s, F16's and B52's together with some British F35s. They are spread through Europe and North America and we have liaised with the Russians. They are covering Eastern Russia and most of Asia down to Australia. As soon as we get notice we will move at breakneck speed!" The General was a cross between enthusiastic and proud. The chance to use nuclear weapons to save human life was almost perfect for him and he intended to be the military commander who made history.

B61s are the primary nuclear gravity bomb of the United States of America. A post Cold War relic, it has since been upgraded and updated with the latest version only a few years old.

"Thanks, keep me updated" The President was sat in his leather chair, cup of freshly brewed coffee in his hand, with his back to the General looking out over the White House lawn, pensive. "Any more casualty updates?"

"Not yet sir" responded the General calmly. It was as if the General was being reminded by the president that human lives were still at the centre of this conflict.

13

Western Russia, Monday 07:00 hrs: Two lone Russian jets on routine patrol sped over fields east of St Petersburg.

"What's that?" One of the pilots had spotted a scorched circular patch in the middle of one of the fields. "I'm sure I saw something in the middle, they looked black and red"

"Are you sure?" Responded the second pilot. "Let's go back and take a closer look. *Control, we've seen something in a field east of St Petersburg. We're going to turn back and take a closer look.*"

The jets banked sharply right as the vapour from their wings drew an almost perfect 'u' in the sky. As they pointed back whence they came, they slowed as much as they could to take a closer look. They were astounded at what they saw.

"Control, we've taken a second look, I think it's them......"

In the middle of the bare patch of field, around a dozen figures appeared to be lounging in the morning sun. Movement was minimal and the pilots only caught a fleeting glimpse but they were very tall and black and red in colour. As the planes flew within a hundred feet of them, the pilots felt a sudden and severe chill through their bodies.

Russian Military Eastern Military District HQ, Khabarovsk, Russia: "Sir, we've found them." The radio operator had burst into the office of the Military District Commander, Colonel General Dmitri Belyaev, something that would normally find him doing extra duties if he was very, very lucky. The General stood up instantly and moved past the front of his desk, discarding his chair as he did so. Unperturbed the radio operator continued "They're in a field East of St Petersburg, we have pilots patrolling the area now, I thought you should know immediately sir."

Belyaev was a veteran of a number of conflicts over his thirty years in the Russian Military and was deemed a trusted ally of the President. As one of five key geographical commanders, the

President had briefed him personally as to what the plan would be should there be a siting of the voyagers. The General sprung into action almost immediately.

"Sir, it's Colonel General Belyaev, we have them sited in a field to the East of St Petersburg, I'm sending the coordinates through now." He had contacted Army General Dominik Volkov, Commander in Chief of the airforce and the man who had ultimate military responsibility for the deployment of tactical nuclear weapons.

"I have the coordinates, expect first contact in the next 15 minutes" his response was short, time was of the essence.

As Army General Volkov put the phone down, a team of Officers contacted ships based in the Baltic Sea and several cruise missiles armed with Kalibr tactical nuclear missiles were launched towards the voyagers.

White House, Washington DC: "Sir, we have a launch!!" The intelligence Colonel, Wesley Miller, had run into the Oval Office with a piece of paper held out in front of him.

Despite Russia and the USA now being allies, the Americans still kept a cautious eye on their Russian counterparts. US satellites had picked up the multiple launches from the Russian northern fleet.

"Where are they headed?"

"In the direction of St Petersburg sir, no confirmation of whether they are conventional weapons or not" With that he ran back out of the office. The President, who stood next to the General, looked across quizzically.

"We're just going to have to wait Mr President" General Carter responded to the question the President didn't need to ask.

Russian Eastern Military District HQ: "Impact in five, four, three, two and one"

The missiles soared through the sky and within metres of the target, the explosives fired, creating a shock wave throughout the warhead. As the core compressed, the resultant fission chain reaction caused a ferocious explosion as they smashed into the ground. The Russian's first deployment of tactical nuclear weapons had commenced.

The two jets pulled back around just as the missiles slammed into the middle of the field. The voyagers were still there immediately prior to impact. Fire gave way to plumes of smoke followed by................an icy cold blast.

"I can confirm the impact exactly where we saw them." Reported the first pilot.

"Can you see them?" Responded control.

"No, just smoke at the............."

Nothing, complete silence.

"Control to fighter 1, come in......"

Nothing.

In St Petersburg, residents going about their business heard several large explosions which drew them out of their properties. As they stood in their gardens, as if waiting for an answer, the temperate morning suddenly gave way to an icy blast, then...........

Nothing.

Quicker than the eye can see, the voyagers had been through the city, leaving nothing in their wake.

The White House, Washington: "The Russians have confirmed the launch of tactical nuclear weapons at an authenticated siting of Voyagers, East of St Petersburg. They've lost contact with the fighters in the area and trying to use satellites to confirm kills, they've asked we do the same to increase chances of success."

"Of course Colonel, anything we can do, they have our full support." The Colonel left the Oval Office. The president was sat on the couch in front of his favourite paintings, opposite his chief of staff. "I've got a really bad feeling about this," he said calmly to his trusted friend.

"I hope you're wrong sir" responded his chief of staff, "but I fear you're not, how long before we will know?"

"About ten minutes I'd say, Joe, this could be the longest ten minutes of our lives."

Ten minutes later......

"That doesn't look good Colonel" The President was referring to the look on his face as he entered the Oval Office with a laptop.

"It's worse sir, 'click' this is St Petersburg just before impact, 'click' and this is five minutes later. It's empty sir, nothing seems to have survived. We have reached out but as I'm sure you can imagine, nothing back at the moment."

"OK, I'll make contact with the Russian President but it seems clear that didn't work, are we sure they just haven't made a mistake with the targeting of the weapons?" Enquired the President desperately.

"I fear not, sir"

Manchester, United Kingdom: "How will we know they're here sir?" Private Dougie Taft was only asking the question everybody else wanted answering but was too afraid to ask. "I mean, I've heard you can't see them and they move so quickly, faster than a bullet?"

"We are still unsure how best we can detect them, we have the best minds working on this" responded Major Tannick. "What we do know is they're very tall, black & red in colour and when they are near, the temperature will drop suddenly and sharply."

"How……how do they kill?"

"To be honest private, nobody knows, no bodies have ever been found"

"So they may still be alive then? Just somewhere else?"

"It's unlikely, look we've got a job to do and we will do it. We need to protect ourselves and our mates so I need you all to switch on."

James was slightly defensive, he didn't know enough and felt he was letting his soldiers down sending them into battle against the unknown. He was addressing the troops in a large warehouse next to the power station, the final speech before they actively deployed. A short while later the Commanding Officer, Lt Col Greaves, dismissed the battalion and they deployed back to their vehicles.

Dougie was 27 years of age and had been in the military for 10 years. Promoted several times, but his frequent misdemeanours meant he was demoted an equal amount and was therefore still at the same rank he joined. A playful character who liked a drink, his sense of fun often became misjudged once alcohol had been added. Married with two young daughters, he had finally realised he was supposed to be a responsible adult, started to adjust his behaviour and had stopped drinking.

Spending more time at home he had become ambitious again and was due to take the junior non-commissioned officer course for the fourth time prior to hopeful promotion. Given his seniority amongst private soldiers, he had taken on the mantle of spokesperson. He climbed into the back of the armoured personnel carrier, a thousand thoughts circling around his head.

"Well, I'm none the wiser, to be honest," Dougie said out loud. The other troops nodded in agreement. They were unusually quiet, focused with a nervous energy. The Warrior armoured carrier housed a section of soldiers with the commander, gunner, driver and four other men, seven in total. It was a snug fit and as a result, they were a tightly knit group.

Dougie was flicking through social media as he sat down. They'd been briefed on the use of mobile phones before deployment and were permitted to use them so long as any geo-locating apps were disabled. "There's a user here that keeps a running total of how many have been killed so far. Says the total is currently over fifty million. God knows how they know that, guessing it's not accurate. Says there's been a few attacks here in the UK, Leeds being one of them........we went near Leeds on the way here!" It had suddenly become very real.

Camp Pendleton, near San Diego, USA: "Oorah!!!!" The Commanding Officer had finished his rousing speech and the Marines gave their familiar war cry before filing out of the hanger. Chad was feeling galvanised and almost ran out of the hangar to his Cougar armoured vehicle together with the other five members of his crew. A short while later, the vehicles filed out of the camp and onto their destination, Diablo Canyon Power Plant, San Luis Obispo County, California. It was a five hour drive at least and would give the Marines plenty of time to ponder how events would transpire.

The White House, Washington DC: "Sir, we have a breakthrough......" The beleaguered intelligence Colonel at last had some good news and it was very much welcomed by all in the Oval Office. "I've had news through that they've managed to isolate strands of DNA and matched them to non-human DNA found at the two crash sites in New York and Tokyo."

The President looked at him knowing he should be pleased but not sure why, sensing he needed help visualising why this was a success, the Colonel continued "It means we can examine them for weaknesses and to understand how they work. We could also hopefully understand how many of them came down to earth, assuming their DNA differs from creature to creature."

"Well that's wonderful news" responded the President, as relieved about the Colonel's detailed explanation as he was about the news itself. "What's the next step?"

"It's early days yet Sir, I'll keep you updated." With that, he left the room as suddenly as he'd entered.

Jet Propulsion Laboratory, California: "We have DNA!!" Debra hollered as she opened the door into the main room to cheering from her colleagues. "It's the first step folks, they've matched some at attack sites to some of the samples we had sent in, we now need to speed up our submissions." There was nodding around the room and a renewed focus as they got back into what they were doing. "I'm proud of what we've done so far, but we've got to keep going, well-done everyone."

Debra had been trying hard to focus on her work and not her family, who she was worried and concerned about having not heard from them for some days now. She had been desperately seeking answers, feeling she was in the middle of this. From 1977 until now her entire life had been shaped by the journey of these two spacecraft, she felt sure that the answer to how these creatures could be defeated was out there, but what was she missing? In her attempt to seek clarity, her mind became more clouded.

Debra walked across to a large chest-high desk in the centre of the room where Jess, amongst others, was busy pulling apart two fused pieces of metal with tweezers. She was in a world of her own and humming quietly to herself, it had taken her several hours to this point and it was how she coped with a mind-numbing task. "Hey Debra, you ok?"

"Sure" responded Debra, "how is it going?"

"I've been working on these two pieces for about five hours now, they're fused together from the heat and I don't want to lose any of the integrity of the structure. Taking on board what you said Debs but we are into some of the really challenging parts of the structure now."

Jesse was working on Voyager 1, now a completely unrecognisable twisted chunk of metal, charred and battered. She looked at the sign hanging down above her head, which identified the spacecraft she was working on, then looked at Debra. "I bet you still remember when this was on Earth the first time, must feel strange being this close now after it travelled so far."

Debra smiled gently, walked over to the coffee machine and wandered back with two freshly brewed coffees. Voyager 1 wasn't directly exposed to the room, it was still inside the large clear glass box and scientists were still using gloves fitted to holes in the glass so they could work on the spacecraft without direct contact. Jess took her hands out of her gloves, wiped them down with a handy wipe, then walked over to a stool next to a nearby table where Debra had put down one of the coffees. Jess was welcome of the break. Sensing that nostalgia had struck a chord with Debra, she continued to quiz her about the launch of Voyager nearly half a century previously. "So, what do you remember? It must have been so exciting, I can't even imagine"

Debra looked back at her as her mind flew back to a far more simple and innocent time, a tear in her eye.

"I remember as if it were yesterday Jess, we were kinda in this room" She paused, looking around as if trying to visualise where it happened. "Of course, it looked nothing like this, for starters the computers were very primitive, that huge window wasn't there, it was pretty dark by comparison. The other difference of course is an almost constant fog of cigarette smoke as pretty much every person that worked in this building smoked."

Jess' face screwed up with disgust at the thought, it was alien for her to pollute her, her fitness was achieved not only through constant training but also by putting the right things into her body. She didn't smoke, drink or eat anything that didn't have the nutritional balance she needed to get the best out of herself, her only vice was coffee and even then she tried to stick to decaf.

"I know Jess, I know what you're thinking" Debrah chuckled "but we knew no better and everybody did it. I haven't smoked for thirty years so don't judge me."

"Haha, I wasn't, I just can't imagine how awful it was"

"Well, it was normal, people smoked in their homes, grocery stores, bars....pretty much every building you went into and it was certainly normal for a place of work to be full of smoke. Anyway, I used to sit over there" Debra pointed to a corner of the room which now contained the water machine. " I remember much more clearly when Voyager 1 was launched over Voyager 2. I was more on the periphery the first time around, at least I felt like I was, The second time though I took it all in. I gave out the nuts before launch, so felt a real part of it all. Of course, I was new, so my involvement was relatively limited."

"Was anybody else who works here now, also working on Voyager?" Asked Jess as she took another sip of her coffee, clasping the mug in both hands.

"No, but there are still plenty around. The main guy, Larry, he now lives in a cottage with his wife in the north of the state. We were very close and I still speak to him from time to time, I really miss him" she paused.

Jess was surprised, Debra never talked about her affection for anybody, she wasn't unfriendly she was just functional and work relationships were just that. No apparent feelings just formal work relationships. This was the first time she had seen Debra's warm, human side.

"I wonder what he's thinking about all this? He's probably the most intelligent and insightful person I've ever had the privilege of meeting, he's in his 90s now." She smiled.

"When you say intelligent, how intelligent?"

"Well, he was obviously academically intelligent, that goes without saying as he had several doctorates by the end of his career, but he had more" Jess tilted her head to one side, as if beckoning her to keep going. "He had academic intelligence and emotional intelligence, he was also capable of theorising far beyond the obvious, I'd love to know what he......" she stopped all of a sudden and looked at Jess. " why haven't I thought of this before?"

"What?"

"Well if anybody knows what is happening and what to do it's Larry. I haven't had a response to my last few texts though"

"Well go and see him, we can cope here, it's not like we don't know what we're doing, if he's as brilliant as you say he is he may just be the answer."

Debra looked at her, trying to think of a reason not to go and see him. In the back of her mind she was worried about why he hadn't been in touch lately, he would usually respond to messages almost instantly. Given his advancing years and of course, the current invasion, she was worried what she would find when she went up there. This was desperate though and she soon put aside her concerns, knowing there was really no other choice.

"You're right Jess, if anybody can stop the killing, it's him. I'll go now." With that, she stood up from her stool, took Jess' now empty mug and walked over to the sink and washed them both. Jess followed her....

"Is there anything you need me to do?" She enquired.

"Just don't tell too many people where I'm going and certainly not who I am going to see. Larry is a living legend in these parts and I don't want to get people's hopes up. He's a lot older obviously and I have no idea how sharp he still is"

Jess smiled and nodded. She found that her hopes had already lifted and didn't want to hear about the possibility that he may have lost some of his sharpness. Debra walked over to her computer, logged out and left the building.

14

Mere human existence was on a precipice, in danger of having inflicted upon us what we had inflicted upon other species throughout time without a second thought. This is how it felt, somewhat surprising was that mankind would be under threat from something outside when it had always been assumed we would destroy ourselves, albeit we perhaps had a hand in our own fate.

Manchester, United Kingdom, Monday, 07:00 hrs: "This is the news at seven, welcome to the BBC, these are the headlines you are waking up to……the unofficial death toll following the Voyager attacks now stands at one hundred and seven million people, including around five million here, in the United Kingdom. The Prime Minister and the war cabinet have moved to a secure bunker underground and the King and the rest of the Royal Family have moved to an undisclosed location outside of London. Russia, having cornered some Voyagers outside of St Petersburg, have used tactical nuclear weapons however were unsuccessful. Electricity is now being rationed across the country with blackouts commonplace, this was due to the attacks on power plants across Europe in general."

Contrary to orders, Private Dougie Taft was watching the BBC app on his phone in the back of his armoured personnel carrier. He had his earbuds in and had turned the volume down so nobody could overhear him. He shuddered as the reports from around the world showed what a desperate and precarious state humans were in. He reflected that, given what humans had done to other animals in hunting them to extinction, we were perhaps getting what we deserved.

"Large-scale looting is now taking place across major towns and cities across the country and the Police are struggling to regain control as the Prime Minister pleads for calm across the population." Footage from a helicopter showed thousands of vehicles attempting to leave major cities across the UK with fires burning in the background. These were from cities that hadn't been attacked and it seemed like what the Voyagers had started, humans were intent on finishing by destroying what was left.

"Sergeant, what do you think will happen next? We've been here for a while now and heard nothing. I mean, the radio has been silent and none of the Battalion has moved so much as an inch."

"I know Dougie but we will get our orders as soon as they are ready, hold your nerve and stay focused. Also, if you think I don't know you're watching TV on that thing then you're as stupid as I thought you were. Take the app off of your phone and show me it before I stick it under the tracks of this vehicle and drive over it" The sergeant's moustache was quivering as he built up into a crescendo of rage.

Dougie deleted the app.

The Whitehouse, Washington DC, several hours later: "So we've established there are around thirty-six of them that we know of and they're split into three groups. One group were last seen here in the States, one in Europe and one in Asia. They are capable of moving around at such great speeds of course so they are just the last locations we have DNA matches on them, they could be anywhere now. What we have discovered, as you know, is there are occasions where they can be seen. An example of this was the now ill-fated tactical nuclear strike just outside St Petersburg, they were seen what looked like basking in a field and were visible for some time. The problem is, even when we can see them we don't know how to neutralise them."

Colonel Miller was once again briefing the President in the Oval Office together with General Carter and the President's Chief of Staff. On order from the President, the Colonel had managed to get some sleep the previous evening and seemed all the fresher for it. The president was sat behind his desk with the General flanking him to his left. The president had attempted to practice what he preached the previous evening and get some sleep but wasn't successful, tossing and turning for a couple of hours before he returned to his office to talk to other world leaders. Several more attacks had been reported overnight, two more in Europe and one in Malaysia.

"No success so far, not one of those things has been killed yet to hundreds of millions of human losses. How much more can we take, they are taking out entire cities and the public has lost confidence." The President slammed the flat of his hand on the table as he spoke "They are now arming themselves and shooting at anybody and anything they think is suspicious. Crime has gone through the roof and civil order is being eroded to the point where we will struggle to continue as a civilised nation. The same is happening across the world. We need a solution and we need it fast." The president appeared calm but focused, he pressed an icon on the control panel on his desk which routed straight through to his secretary "Can you get me the Russian President and the Secretary General of NATO please?"

Pasadena, California: Debra had decided to rest overnight before she made her way North up the Route 101 to see Larry. Los Angeles was becoming very precarious as the rule of law hung by a thread so she aimed to avoid the City and had plotted an alternative route. In fact, she aimed to avoid any major cities and this had turned the already long ten-hour journey into one that would likely take two days.

Debra had decided to plan for the worst and had packed for most eventualities. As a young girl, she enjoyed camping in the Appalachian Mountains in New England and, as she placed her well-loved roll-up sleeping bag into the back of her car, she felt a warm wave wash over her emotionally as she remembered those trips with her parents. They would pack their station wagon with so much equipment that Debra could hardly fit in, having to crawl into a small space surrounded by sleeping bags, pots and pans ready for the journey up into the mountains and the adventures therein.

She grabbed her 'Greenville' sweat top from her cupboard as she left her house, another reminder of happier times. Being an only child, her parents had often given Debra the opportunity to bring a friend with her on their many trips, but she didn't want anybody else there. Her parents were the centre of her world and she didn't need any other company. As she pulled out of her driveway and switched the radio on, she was soon snapped out of her nostalgic journey as reality kicked back in with a news update 'Is this the end of humanity?' Asked the radio presenter for probably the twentieth time that day. Debra adjusted her rearview mirror and edged out of her drive and onto the main road.

New York City: "David, I want to leave, I don't feel safe here any more." David and Lizzie had remained in Manhattan since Voyager 1 was discovered as they struggled to find transport to take them home. David was also cognisant of the stories filtering out through social media of vehicles being taken at gunpoint as New Yorkers' desperate attempts to get out of the city escalated into violence.

"Look, we are going to struggle to get out in one piece, the kids are safe so we just need to be patient and wait for the right opportunity to get out. We've got a place to stay and we have money so we can afford to wait. New York has already been attacked, surely if there was anything else for them, they would have taken it at the same time?"

"I admire your faith, I just want to go honey, please get us out of here" she pleaded as she tugged at his arm, she had been talking to Ethan and Emily by phone earlier that day and her need to be with them was never higher despite the fact they were much safer where they were.

The couple were walking along 34th Street, past 6th Avenue and were approaching the Empire State Building. They had spent most of the previous days in the hotel room watching the news as it rolled through but were now suffering from 'cabin fever'. The last straw was when one of the news channels added a red box with a number in the top left corner of the screen to show how many were confirmed dead. It looked like a sick totaliser of the type shown on charity and fundraising shows to indicate total funds raised, they decided they needed to get away from it.

As they walked towards the giant Art Deco building, most of the shops they passed were either closed or boarded up. The odd food truck was still operating and some were doing roaring trade as they saw their competition almost disappear in an instant.

"We should eat" David could smell melted, shredded Mozzarella cheese and tomato sauce which meant only one thing, fresh New York pizza. As they followed their noses around the corner they found a small metal cart with a parasol above it. The line was several deep and the vendor was struggling to make it quickly enough to meet demand.

"Wow, thirteen bucks for a slice?! Clearly, somebody is profiting from this disaster."

"Come on David, I'm not going to be a part of that. That's extortion and taking advantage of desperation, I'm disgusted."

Lizzie was upset at the obviously desperate families, including young children, who were pushing and jostling each other in the queue.

"Honey, we don't know when we will get to eat a warm meal again, let's just spend the money." He looked longingly at her, his stomach noises reminding them both that there was no time to lose.

"Ok fine, smelling this I'm getting hungry too......" she suddenly tensed up, looked up then around her "Did you feel that?!"

"Yeah I did, that was freezing, exactly like Central Park."

"What shall we do?" pleaded Lizzie, as her eyes widened with fear. Nobody else had noticed, having not felt it before, as they talked in hushed tones. Then, as soon as it came, it went.

The Whitehouse, Washington DC: The president was on a conference call with the other NATO leaders. "We have to be prepared to commit significant forces should there be another siting of Voyagers. Our intelligence is telling us that one group has been seen in Russia, probably the same group which struck in St Petersburg. We now have at least half a dozen sittings of them between St Petersburg in the North and Smolensk further South.

They seem to be visible most of the time now and we have noted that they do change colours from time to time, for example on one occasion they seem to have a blue hue to them."

"When were they last seen?" enquired the French President.

"Within the last hour. We have drones, satellites, aircraft you name it and it's up there. I'm confident we will pin them down. We've got to gamble and I think the time to do that is now. I've spoken to the Russian President and he is willing to deploy significant numbers of Russian Military in the West of their country, he's invited us to join them and work together. I took the liberty of agreeing subject to you ratifying that decision during this conversation."

There was silence from the other leaders as they took in the request. Under normal circumstances, the President would have worked in the background to garner support before this conversation had taken place, but he didn't have the time.

"The rough plan, which will need to be significantly refined, is to commit considerable assets to the far west of Russia. Once our resources identify the voyagers again we attack with the full might of our joint alliance. We will be supported by the full array of military aircraft and naval ships located in the Caspian Sea."

The German Chancellor unmuted his microphone. Germany had been hit by a number of attacks and with tens of millions dead in his country, the populous had started to blame his government for a lack of action.

"I am not a gambling man, Mr President." He said slowly and calmly. "But is it wise to commit such a large proportion of our forces to one attack when we don't actually know what it takes to kill them?"

"Chancellor, I understand your reluctance, but we are on the precipice. If we don't destroy them soon it may be too late."

"I am not reluctant Mr President, just careful"

"I understand, so that's the question. Will you all ratify my decision to commit significant NATO Forces to support Russia in the West of their country? This will be subject to a full plan currently being worked through jointly by Generals from all sides."

His mouth was dry as nerves set in. He believed this was the right way to go but it relied on total agreement and there were a number of characters, some less affected by the voyagers up to this point than others. Uncomfortable with the silent wall in front of him, he started to fill in the blanks.

"We have enacted an old Cold War protocol which effectively turns a large part of Germany into a landing zone. We will soon have troop carriers landing every 15 minutes having been transported from the US. I am confident that, within twenty-four hours, we will have around half a million military personnel making their way across Europe and into Russia, but we can't do this alone."

Still silent

"The future of humanity is in our hands, we have a responsibility to the people of the world to be brave"

The British Prime Minister cut across him. "We're in…."

"So are we" revealed the German chancellor

"Us too," said the French President.

One by one all of the NATO leaders agreed that, together with Russia, they would commit several million personnel to Western Russia in an attempt to take out one of the three pods (this is how the collective was now commonly referred to) of Voyagers and end the threat they posed. As for the rest of them? They hadn't thought that far forward.

The president ended the video conference. "Wow, I thought they weren't gonna agree there, we need this to work General" The

President was wiping beads of sweat from his brow with his overworked handkerchief as he spoke to his senior military advisor.

"Don't worry sir, we are already working on the plan, this will make 'shock and awe' look like 'knock and bore'" he smiled to himself, pleased with his little attempt at humour, it was completely missed.

"Just make sure it works General, or we're screwed!" the President barked.

15

Russia, Tuesday, 07:00 hrs: Military ships poured into the Black Sea like ants crawling out of an anthill when reacting to an attack on their nest. Navies from Countries more comfortable as enemies were working together to dock in ports around the North East of this huge transition point from Europe to Asia, from East to West. Tanks and armoured vehicles sped off the ships and headed straight for mass convoys heading towards Western Russia and their starting point for the great battle ahead. Greeks and Turks, Russians and Ukrainians, NATO and Russia, all as one.

The routes had been marked out by Military Police and all tank commanders had to do was follow the route signs given to them. The various routes had animals allocated to differentiate from one another. The Greek Military were following 'route wolf' towards the battlefront and their German made Leopard 2 main battle tanks looked mean and threatening. They let out a deep guttural gargle as their massive diesel engines kicked back into life, thrusting them forward with such force, that it physically pushed the main gun into the air.

"Route Wolf, Vasilis. I'll give you a clue, it looks like a big dog" Vasilis Oikonomou had been a tank driver for several years and was well-liked by his crew, but he was often the butt of jokes and today was no different. Whilst good at driving the huge German behemoth, he was often slow on the uptake and needed a little more direction than most. They were first off the ship and Vasilis was desperately looking for the sign that marked the beginning of the route.

"I can't see it, why must they always hide these signs where they are hard to find? I can feel everybody behind me getting annoyed now" His battle helmet was on lop-sided and it was no wonder he couldn't see as one of his eyes was almost completely covered by his head gear.

"Listen, stop worrying, I can see some signs in the distance beyond the crossroad, that must be them" responded the tank commander,

Yianis, "just drive forward and if it's not them we can figure out our next move there, at least the others will be off the ship" with that, Vasilis moved the tank forward and through the first junction where he picked up the first sign for 'route wolf'.

The Hellenic (Greek) Army was landing in the Black Sea resort city of Sochi with both port and airport being used to bring in troops and logistical equipment together with tanks and other armour. It was a spectacular site as tanks and heavy machinery were driven along motorways in Sochi to huge fields with railway sidings outside the city where they were placed onto trains which would send them closer to the action. Across the Black Sea American, Turkish, Spanish, Italian, Portuguese and French Armour was being unloaded and out onto trains as further reinforcements arrived at Airports. It was a mass movement of militaries unseen since the Second World War. Except this time their enemy was not each other, it wasn't human at all. To the far North West, the British, German, Polish, American and many other NATO forces were heading East across Europe to join them.

"So, how many are there?" Asked Vasilis, as he strapped the tracks onto the train carriage. "There must be millions of them"

"Not many, but they've already killed millions in Russia, so they are lethal. Just look at what we have here and we are just a fraction of what will confront them." Responded Yianis as he stood next to the sidings, busily puffing away on his cigarette.

"How long will we be here?"

"As long as it takes" Yianis was barely paying attention to him as he flicked through the news on his phone. 'No more attacks of late' he thought to himself, he was beginning to wonder if they were still around, how did they know where they were? It wouldn't be long before he would be fully briefed and find the answer to that question.

New York City: "Why do you watch that? You know it's not going to be good news.... Honey, are you listening to me" David was staring blankly at the TV in the hotel, not really taking in what the news was telling him. "Honey?"

"Sorry, I was just thinking, we could have died in Central Park.....you know, when Voyager crashed. They were obviously there"

"But they weren't" interrupted Lizzie, "they weren't and we are still here, please don't overthink this, we still have a lot to do to get out of New York and back home. I need you to be strong David, can you do that for me?"

David looked over from his armchair next to the bed, where Lizzie had propped herself up on four pillows, tears welling in his eyes.

"Ok.......ok, I'll try better. I just want out of here and back with our babies"

"So do I and we will, now, stop watching that and come over here." David turned the volume on the television down to a whisper and wandered over to her, kicking off his shoes as he crawled onto the massive hotel bed. He pushed an icon on the iPad set into the wall next to the bed to dim the lights and they held each other tightly and wept. In the background pictures of millions of military and their vehicles were being shown travelling towards the Western planes of Russia.

Jet Propulsion Laboratory, California: Voyager 2 had finally arrived from Japan, delivered via a Chinook helicopter an hour previously. Gus continued to carefully separate parts of the newly arrived spacecraft in the same way he had with the first one. In the background, the twenty-four-hour news continued to play.

"Voyagers move at terrific speed. They are almost impossible to see when moving and the only way to know they are coming is to look around at the effect they have on objects when they move. Across the sea or open water, the surface is whipped as they pass over it, painting patterns that would be beautiful if not so ominous. Across the land they are less obvious and often are not seen until they are on top of their target, even then they can't easily be seen, leaving devastation in their path. They appear to have arrived on Earth without craft having travelled at great speeds across the solar system. When they do stop their form becomes more obvious and their skin loses its translucent form."

The presenter looked to be enjoying his part in what seemed like, a science fiction drama. He was interviewing a Professor from Harvard University and the Professor was summing up his thoughts on the Voyagers.

"Without eyes in the way animals on earth have eyes, they look as fearful as they are lethal. Standing around 8 feet tall and without most recognisable facial features, their skin has four small holes across the length of their head with what appears to be a light liquid film across the top. Whilst they appear to float a couple of feet up, it's more likely that the bottom of their body is just not visible to the human eye, with their imprint seen on the ground. Their skin does not remain one colour but instead, it appears to change depending on where they are with no consistent colour across their body at any one time, they can have a dark blue upper torso and a dark red lower torso for example. Just before they kill, they become visible and change to a dark red colour with black stripes. They are completely silent and when they kill, nothing is left behind, a lightning attack where the human body is just disintegrated. They don't appear to be solid and can pass through buildings, vehicles, trees and anything that gets in their way, at speed. Truly awesome opponents capable of annihilating the human race with relative ease." The two men continued to theorise about these awesome creatures with a ticker in the top corner of the screen continuing to count the dead like it was some sort of sick game show.

"But why are there Voyagers on Earth? Why do such awesome beings feel the need to come to our planet and rip from us everything we hold so dear?" The presenter continued to ask. These were the exact thoughts going through Gus's mind as he continued his meticulous examination of the Voyager 2 spacecraft.

16

Western Russia, Wednesday, 06:00 hrs: It was an amazing sight. Across the flat planes of Western Russia stood the combined armies of NATO and Russia. Over 10,000 tanks, thousands of artillery pieces and three million soldiers. In the Caspian Sea were submarines ready to fire cruise missiles. They were ready.

Five miles across the planes were voyagers, about a dozen in total and representing one of the three pods of creatures known to be on the planet. They were visible and not really moving as they sat in the mid-morning sun, seemingly oblivious to the one hundred NATO and Russian Divisions that lay a few miles West formed into twenty Army Groups each Commanded by a five-star General. The biggest formation since World War Two with more firepower available to it than any of the major powers across both world wars. A truly formidable site and one that only a few years earlier nobody would have thought likely.

"But how do you fight something you can't see?" A question that Corporal Steve Matthews was asking of his Sergeant. Steve was a 23-year-old with five years of service, married with a three-year-old son whom he doted on. A soldier in the British Light Infantry he had never seen active service and this was his first taste of action. Of course, he'd seen on TV what had happened over the last few days but he couldn't help but feel impressed by the might of the military forces that had been drawn together, it gave him real confidence.

Steve was sat in the back of a Warrier Armoured Personnel Carrier with the door wide open letting in the cool air of the Russian day. The rest of his section were also in the Armoured Personnel Carrier and morale was decidedly high given recent events with most thinking they were going to annihilate the enemy in no time at all. Steve had a tiny shred of doubt, characterised by a dead feeling in the pit of his stomach, which he couldn't shake. What had happened in New York and Tokyo had been the subject of significant censorship and it had made Steve question why.

"Don't worry yourself, Steve, just worry about the week in Cyprus we have been promised to decompress when this is all over, it's going to be hot and messy over there" The Sergeant smiled as he patted Steve on the back and winked.

The inside of the carrier was cramped, unsurprisingly dark green and had a smell of oil familiar to anybody who has served in the forces. Soldiers sat on two benches which ran the length of the carrier and were attached to the inside left and right sides of the vehicle. There was chatter on the radio which seemed positive as the various Commanders passed on formation information and ensured that there was complete coordination across the vast armies which now stretched from just outside Smolensk in the North to Kursk in the South, a distance of around 310 miles.

Thirty miles south was the imposing figure of a Greek, Leopard 2 main battle tank, exhaust spewing a dark grey cloud into the morning air as it started up. "Well, you got us here......eventually" Yianis was still far from impressed at the dressing down he had received from the squadron commander because they had managed

244

to get lost en route to their Form Up Point (FUP), from where they would commence their part of the attack. And by them, it was Vasilis.

"It looked like a dog, it's not my fault the drawing was bad" reasoned Vasilis.

"Two things, firstly, every other tank in the world has managed to get to their starting point on time and without getting lost" he raised his eyebrows as he spoke with stern authority.

"Secondly, it says wolf underneath it......in Greek!!" The signs were in Greek and English as this was their assigned route.

Vasilis sat back and pondered a response before deciding that silence may be the most effective way to stop the telling off. Fortunately, all of the arguing had made him forget about the precarious position they found themselves in.

With troops from the USA, Russia, France, UK, Germany, Poland, Canada, Australia and the Netherlands, it was important that all forces acted as one and therefore answered to one Commander at the top, Field Marshall Sir William Redmonshire from the United Kingdom.

Sir William was based in Poland with his team of Generals from the various army groups and between them, they had planned and would coordinate the attack against this formidable foe. Satellite images were beamed live to the command centre and decisions were made which were fed out to the various commanders in the field. The latest images still showed the Voyagers static in fields to the northeast of Betlitsa.

Cognisant of the previous encounters, the plan was to pummel the Voyagers with artillery and cruise missiles and then attack them with wave after wave of infantry with the assumption being made that the Voyagers would not be capable of killing all of them. There would be considerable losses but the Commanders felt sure they would be ultimately successful.

"This is zero calling all army groups on this channel, please confirm in number order you are receiving me" The HQ radio operator had a tough task to pull together this international military force, the accepted language was English.

"Hello zero this is Army Group 1" responded an American voice, "receiving you loud and clear".

"Hello zero this is Army Group 2" a thick French accent responded, *"receiving over"*.

This continued across all 20 Army Groups in turn. Steve Matthews was in the British Army Group which was Army Group 7 and listened intently as each of the 20 groups responded. Vasilis was in Army Group 11, a joint Greek, Turkish and Spanish Army Group.

They tried hard to visualise just how numerous the forces were but couldn't imagine what three million people looked like, on top of that were the artillery, navy, air forces etc. mind-blowing.

"This is zero calling all call signs, stand by." The naval callsigns were on a separate channel to prevent congestion.

"Zero to all naval call signs, commence targeted attack, you have the coordinates" With that, submarines and naval ships launched a barrage of cruise missiles.

Missiles shrieked across the sky and headed towards their targets, hundreds of miles away. Second after second, more and more were launched and thousands of vapour trails decorated the horizon.

As they neared the targets the HQ operator got back on the radio.

"Hello all artillery callsigns this is zero, commence artillery bombardment"

Soldiers hauled giant artillery shells into field guns as thousands of artillery and rocket launch systems dispensed their munitions towards the same targets. The blue sky was crisscrossed with the vapour from the rockets and shells. The sound of the artillery shells rhythmically thumped the air, every few seconds. As rockets flew overhead they sucked the air from around them.

Steve Matthews was astounded by the power and might of what they had unleashed.....

Then came the order......" *all army groups, advance!!!*"

There was a short jerk as the Armoured Personnel Carrier moved forward, then it moved more smoothly. Vasilis' Leopard tank also quickly accelerated, dragging tonnes of metal and ordnance with it. Millions of men and women all moving towards the targets.

"Can I get an update on the targets?" Asked Field Marshall Redmonshire.

"There's too much smoke and debris at the moment sir, but I can confirm 95% of the munitions hit the target area." There was a cheer around the room.........and then it began.

Steve was listening as the confirmation came through, his mind drifted to his wife and child and looked forward to being reunited with them. He looked towards his Sergeant and said "Sarge, how lon…………………………..

Vasilis Leopard 2, was speeding towards its target. Yianis looked across at his driver and shouted "You'd better not get us lost this ti…………..

Back in HQ, the Field Marshall asked for an update on the armoured formations.

"Hello Army Group One, this is zero. Can I have an update please?"

Nothing.

"Hello Army Group One, this is zero. Update please, over"

Nothing

"Try Army Group Two!" The Field Marshall was no longer calm.

"Hello Army Group Two, this is zero. Update please, over"

Nothing

"Any callsigns on this group, can I get a radio check, over"

Nothing

"I think the radio is broken" shouted the operator. He was interrupted by the intelligence officer.

"Sir, you'd better take a look at these," he said as he handed his tablet with fresh satellite images over to the Field Marshall.

"What am I looking at, there's nothing there?" Demanded the Field Marshall.

"Minutes ago, sir, that was our Army" came the response. He pinched the screen and opened his fingers out, to reveal a blurred figure, black and red in colour.

At the front of the formations, all they saw was dust, felt a sharp temperature change then nothing. Nothing was left. Three million people annihilated. Three million fathers, mothers, brothers, sisters, sons and daughters, annihilated.

Thinking on his feet the radio operator tried again. *"Any artillery units on this channel, radio check, over"* They were located further back than the main bulk of the force so may still be alive.

Nothing. Nothing had survived……..

The White House, Washington DC: "Mr President, it's General Carter on the phone for you" The president's chief of staff beckoned urgently.

The Chief of Staff was walking across the Oval Office with the secure phone in his hand. The President looked pleased "Ahh" he mouthed as he took the phone "this must be an update". The President had asked the head of the US Armed Forces, General Carter, for an update as soon as some progress had been made and he assumed this was good news.

"Michael, give me some good news!" He said, smiling as he spoke to the General. As the Presidents Chief of Staff slowly watched, the smile disappeared from his face, turning to horror before all of the colour in his face wash away.

"Wh....what?! All of them? No survivors at all? But how? How can that have happened?" The President stumbled back into his chair. President Williams was not a man predisposed to drama, his chief of staff and friend knew this was bad, very bad.

"Mr President, are you ok? Sir.......Jim, Jim it's me are you ok?" The president just sat in his chair, looking at his phone in horror. General Carter could be heard at the other end of the phone but the

President was unresponsive. "Jim!!" Shouted the Chief of Staff. Suddenly, as quickly as the trance began, it finished.

The President picked up his phone and spoke to General Carter once again. "General, I take it this will be common knowledge across all of our nations shortly? I must address the American people, they can't find this out from someone else, this is my responsibility".

He thanked the General and terminated the call. He looked up at his Chief of Staff. "Joe, I need to address the nation, I have some news" sensing the news wasn't good, Joe responded "how many, sir?"

"All of them, every god damn one of them, three million….half of them American, gone. This should be the worst news I can deliver but it's not"

"What do you mean?" Queried Joe, shock imprinted on his face.

"The Voyagers are still out there Joe, they've just wiped out one of the largest forces ever assembled with the most modern technology available to us, then walked away without a scratch. How do I tell the public that? I don't want to start a blind panic, but I have to be honest." Clearly panicked, the President was talking quickly.

"Can you schedule an address to the nation for this evening? In the mean time I need a conference call with the other world leaders so I can at least give the public an idea of how we are going to get out of this. I need General Carter to talk to his counterparts and what the hell are NASA doing?! These things have come from space, I want every person in NASA working on what they are, where they came from and what the hell we are going to do to defeat them!" The President was understandably a mixture of angry, upset and scared.

"Yes sir" replied Joe, he then swiftly left the office to instruct his team and ensure all that was needed by the President, was done as quickly and efficiently as possible.

As he did so, the president stood in the Oval Office, looking out of the window and onto the lawns beyond. He was thinking about the great loss the nation had just experienced and the responsibility he felt. But he knew he needed to snap out of it, it wasn't dramatic to suggest that the fate of human kind may depend on it.

17

The Pentagon, Arlington County, Virginia, a short while later: General Carter had made a short journey across Washington DC to the relative safety and comfort of his own office. He preferred to make military calls out of the earshot of the President, it prevented what he saw as silly questions. He was on a conference call with his military counterparts in NATO, Russia, China, Japan and India. His head of intelligence, Colonel Wesley Miller, was giving the latest update

"As you know, the low yield nuclear option has had no impact at all, if anything they seem to be getting stronger. They instantly know when and where we move our assets and neutralise them. We are down to four carrier groups, two American, one British and one Chinese. If we carry on as we have been they will be gone within the next 24 hours. Our satellites have tracked a buildup of voyagers in and around the United Kingdom, the United States and Russia. They move so quickly we can't track their speed, gravity seems to have no effect on them."

"How many casualties in total?" Snapped General Carter.

"It's hard to give an accurate number sir bu…."

"Cut the bullshit son, how many casualties!!!" Interrupted the General

"It's in the hundreds of millions sir" responded Colonel Miller, voice starting to tremble a little under pressure.

General Lui Xu Ping from the Chinese Peoples Liberation Army was listening through a headset to a translation of the conversation into Mandarin. He spoke and understood perfect English but refused to show that in public, seeing it as a weakness. He stood up, meaning that the top of his head could no longer be seen on the screen.

"Hundreds of millions?!" he exclaimed in perfect English. "What is the remaining strength of the military?" He asked.

"Our best estimates are that NATO is now at around 40%, China around the same with Russia at 30% and India and Japan around 35%. This is changing by the minute, the speed of the enemy is such that we could be all but wiped out now and we just wouldn't know it". Responded Colonel Miller.

"Our militaries have less than 24 hours before they are annihilated, humanity probably has only a few days.......now is a damn good time to talk if you have any idea how we are going to solve this gentlemen!" Barked General Carter, he tapped his camera as he shouted down the microphone. "I think we have nothing to lose, we shouldn't discount using the nuclear option again. I understand the only time they are still long enough is when they are in a large city and if we don't do it then when can we? We can't discount that the reason it didn't work last time was that they moved. Which large cities are they near Colonel?"

"Sir, the closest city to any voyager threats at this time is New York, bu......"

"How long would it take to evacuate the city?" General Carter seemed focused all of a sudden.

"Well sir, as you know, the city has been hit hard by voyagers in the last 24 hours and what is left of the population has been doing everything they can to get out of there since. We still estimate there are around 2 million in the city and we would struggle to get most of those out if there is another attack in the next 12 hours" responded Colonel Miller.

General Sir Michael Edwards was the British Chief of the General Staff. A third generation general, privately educated and incredibly sharp, he had a reputation for being straight to the point. "General Carter, are you suggesting that you are going to nuke one of your own cities, kill millions of your own people, using a tactic that based on all of the evidence we have so far won't work?!"

" yes sir, that's exactly what I'm suggesting" responded General Carter. He had a reputation for being headstrong regardless of the consequences and was very much living up to that. "I will arrange a meeting with the President shortly and explain the plan. That is…..unless any of you have a better idea"

General Lui Xu Ping unmuted his microphone and all eyes became focused on him. "Whilst in the past I would have been happy to see large parts of North America wiped out, now I'm not so sure. Also, what happens if the next city they appear near is Beijing? What price are we willing to pay for victory…….if it even works?"

The White House, Washington DC, Wednesday, 21:00 hrs: the President was in the Oval Office, sat opposite his senior military advisor on the sofas.

"Sir, I've spoken to NATO Generals and those of other contributing nations and we are beginning to come to the conclusion that there is one option we haven't tried yet." General Carter was again talking to the President, who now appeared a little calmer and considerably more focused. As a religious man, he had prayed for strength and spoken to the First Lady and now realised it was his time to step up to the plate.

"Go on General, what do you think?" Asked the President.

"Well, we've thrown a considerable arsenal at them, tonnes of explosives and ordinance. None of it has had any effect, nothing at all. We think we've exhausted our conventional options......." General Carter was interrupted.

"General, you're not going to say what I think are you? We have just lost the equivalent of the population of Philadelphia, all gone, and you are seriously suggesting we use strategic nukes?"

"Sir, I know how unpalatable that sounds but the voyagers are powerful beyond anything we've ever seen. They travel at speeds beyond anything we can comprehend, they can move without being seen and through all of this, they haven't been so much as scratched." The General was pleading with the leader of the free world.

"We could use tactical nuclear weapons and keep the impact of them relatively localised, we could pummel them when they are still and we can see them. The problem is the Russians tried that and it didn't work, they got stronger if anything. There's really only one option left sir, strategic nuclear weapons."

"What?!"

"I know sir, but I don't think we have much choice. We will need to move very quickly so I'll need you to pre-authorise the use of American weapons but the British, French, Chinese and Russians seem confident they will get authorisation." The president looked pensive. "Sir......this is like no threat any human has ever faced, it's potentially an extinction event"

"Thanks General, I have a meeting with other world leaders in an hour, I'll let you know what we agree. Really useful to get an idea of what you're all thinking. Forgive me, I must go as I need to speak with NASA before the meeting". The General stood up and left the room.

The President walked between the two patterned cream sofas in the office and towards the wall. He moved over to the large paintings which adorn the Oval Office, in particular the paintings of President Franklin D Roosevelt, George Washington and Abraham Lincoln. 'What would they think of this?' he wondered, 'what would they do?' He had always felt that he was in the privileged position he was because of the brilliance of his predecessors and would often look at those pictures in wonderment at what they had seen and done in their times as President.

He walked over to the door, opened it and asked the secretary if she would fetch him a strong coffee. Joe was standing outside having just put the phone down. "Joe, I'm getting an update from NASA and there's a couple of things I'd like to talk through with you if you don't mind. I could use a second opinion" Whilst under such pressure, it was almost a surprise the President was still so polite.

Both men walked back into the Oval Office and sat on the sofas. Fresh coffee was brought in and the President shared with his chief of staff the update he had just received from General Carter. Joe's eyes widened as he ran through the options as they'd been spelled out to him.

"So, that's where we are. The NASA Administrator is phoning in the next five minutes. I can't help thinking that they may hold the key to defeating these things. My fear is that we are going to end up unleashing a nuclear Armageddon as we try and defeat the undefeatable. I'm conflicted Joe, my instinct is to stall and play for time, but what am I playing? I don't know who our adversary is let alone their capabilities or intention and we certainly can't negotiate with it."

Joe stared into the eyes of the President, he felt that he needed to respond but didn't know what to say. The options were all unpalatable and he could see the President was genuinely torn. He glanced down at his mug of coffee on the table, picked it up, looking into the swirling dark hot liquid. 'It's funny how interesting something as inanimate as coffee can suddenly seem so interesting' he thought to himself. He smelled the fresh coffee beans as he took a long and satisfying sip. As he gulped it down, he drew his gaze back up to that of the president.

"Sir, you're a good man and this is the most difficult decision anybody in your position has ever made." He looked up at the paintings of previous presidents as he said it. "But I know that whatever decision you make will be the right one. And whatever you decide......." He paused.

"What, Joe?......" replied the President.

"Whatever you decide, I'll be right behind you, regardless of the consequences."

The president breathed out, looked down and then slowly back up fixing the gaze of his trusted friend. "Thanks, Joe, I needed to hear that." A gentle smile spread across his face and his eyes looked relieved.

"Sir, it's NASA….." another assistant walked in with a phone. The President walked across, took the phone and sat back on the sofa. He looked at the handset and pressed the speaker icon.

"Brad, it's the President and you're on speaker phone with my chief of staff here too. He can hear anything we talk about"

"Of course, sir." Responded the most senior person at NASA.

"Bill, this is serious, I'm going to brief you on what I know then I need you to do the same". The President proceeded to fully update the NASA administrator on what had happened in Western Russia. Bill remained completely silent on the other end of the phone to the extent the President had to check he was still there on a couple of occasions. "And that's it, Bill, you now know what I know. What I don't know is, what these things are and where did they come from and I need you to get that for me. I can't think of any other department better equipped to answer that than yours. I want your best minds focused on this and it goes without saying that anything you need, you'll get."

"Thank you, sir. One theory we are testing is that they used Saturn's largest moon, Titan to form a kinda bridge to earth. We don't yet understand why or how but we are looking at that. We have the two Voyager spacecraft at the Jet Propulsion Laboratory in California and our scientists are examining those for clues. I'll be honest though sir, science doesn't work as quickly as you probably need. We may get an answer for you as to what these are but that may take years….."

"You've got twelve hours Bill" The President was curt. "I am being asked to make a decision that could spell the end of mankind as we know it, tell me what you need."

The NASA man didn't seem confident, he knew they could get some answers but, whilst they probably had the first interactions with the Voyagers, he wasn't convinced they were best placed to give quick time intelligence and information to the President that would enable him to make a decision. The scientist wasn't used to working this way and didn't feel comfortable at all.

As soon as he put the phone down the President walked into his bathroom and washed his face. He was perspiring profusely and needed to cool down. He physically felt the stress, felt the pressure. As he dried his face he could feel his heart pounding as his blood pressure rose. 'This isn't helping' he thought to himself. He gently laid the soaked towel down next to the sink, looked up at himself and exhaled before returning to his office where General Carter was now waiting.

Colonel Miller entered the Oval Office. "We have them sir"

"What do you mean have them?" responded the President.

"They are in Battery Park, South Manhattan."

"We need to take them out sir!" General Carter interjected.

"Yes, thank you General" The President responded, rapidly losing patience with his most senior Military Officer. "How long have they been there?"

"From what we can tell they've been there all morning, they seem to be basking in the sun, largely visible. The roads and surrounding area have all been cordoned off so nobody is anywhere near them." Responded the Colonel.

"Ok, we need to be in a position to act decisively, General, how are our forces looking in the area?"

"About 15,000 in the near vicinity but we could move more up should you require it, sir"

"Yes please" responded the President, "we will win this by taking risks, of that I'm sure. Get what you can up to New York and be ready to move on the targets"

"Affirmative sir, I'll inform you when completed" with that the General turned around and left the Oval Office. The President picked up one of the a4 size photographs Colonel Miller had printed out. It looked to have been taken by a drone and was relatively clear. The voyagers had a blue hue to them and appeared to be lying horizontally looking towards the camera, but nobody knows how they function so it may well be they couldn't see or hear the drone.

Diablo Canyon Power Plant, San Luis Obispo County, California, Thursday 06:00 hrs: Chads Cougar armoured vehicle was parked up in a field to the north of the power plant. The location was teaming with US Marines and Chad was standing outside of his vehicle looking down at a screen which showed most of the deployed troops through the main camera of the drone which Chad was currently operating. It was a task he very much enjoyed as it fulfilled the inner child in him, it was like playing with a big toy. As the drone flew between the giant concrete domes, he smiled broadly as it banked steeply through a small gap, he was having so much fun that he almost forgot the desperate position humanity was in. The hot morning sun provided a useful backlight as he watched his colleagues shrink on his screen as the drone soared higher, his radio crackled back into life.

"All units, stand by for a sitrep………all units are to move to Santa Maria Airport, you will then be airlifted to New York JFK airport where you will receive further orders. Officers to be briefed further at Santa Maria, Alpha Company have the grid reference and will lead the convoy. That is all…..out."

Chad looked at his crewmates, shrugged his shoulders and carefully guided the drone back to his location, landing it neatly in front of him. He then got back into his vehicle, sparking the Cougar back into life a short while later. "New York? Really?" He was confused as to why they were being moved so far away from California, maybe the rumours about troop shortages were right?

The White House, Washington DC: "Well given the direction of travel, we think Newark Energy Centre is their most obvious target, but they could be looking more generally at Southern Manhattan."

"So you don't know then, Colonel" the President was losing patience but it wasn't the Colonels fault and he knew it. "That was unfair Wes, I apologise, keep going" The President was not wearing his tie and jacket and was stood over his giant desk, shirt sleeves rolled up, in the Oval Office having dashed in from his living quarters.

"Thank you, sir, looking at the reports we have there is intelligence from a number of sources that sudden drops in temperature were felt as far up as Central Park then followed a line down the city with the last reports near Battery Park itself. It's safe, therefore, to assume that's the route they have taken. If they move as the crow flies, which we assume they do, they are heading in a line southwest of the city. The obvious power source in that direction is Newark, as I said."

"Thank you Colonel.....General, where are we with reinforcements?"

"Well, we have a number of Battalions of Marines on their way to back up what was already in place around the city. I do have to tell you sir, it leaves other sites vulnerable."

"I know, it's a risk we have to take." He nodded at the Military Commanders as he straightened his back and they left the room. He followed shortly after, walking straight to the Cabinet Room.

In the Cabinet Room, the President was briefing the rest of his Government. As he went through the options he could read what they were all thinking. The gravity of the situation was perfectly summed up by the speaker of the house when she said "Sir, we understand what you're asking us but I can't see an answer that doesn't kill our own people." It was perfectly true. The only thing that was guaranteed was further innocent people being killed. Further than that, a strategic nuclear strike would effectively destroy New York, rendering it uninhabitable for many years. The president ended the meeting and decided it was time for some rest.

He walked out of the cabinet room and then made his way towards the residential portion of the White House. He had learned during his distinguished military career that he should always get some sleep when he can as you never know when the next opportunity will be. As he entered the West Sitting Hall he caught a glimpse of the First Lady in the kitchen. He had been married to Sherri for 34 years and she was his rock, he was relieved to see her.

"Hey......" he smiled at her as she fixed his gaze. She was in her night dress and gown and had been making herself a sandwich. Still down to earth regardless of the position they held, she treated the residential quarters of the White House like a real household. She insisted on cleaning and maintaining this area like you would your own home. She wouldn't allow housekeepers to work in the area and insisted on making all decorative decisions herself. For her this was about maintaining a semblance of normality in an otherwise abnormal existence. She did this for herself but more importantly for their two children, Max and Jessica. It was important to Sherri that they had as normal an upbringing as possible and she wasn't going to let her husbands position or her responsibilities as First Lady get in the way of that.

"Hey….." she smiled back at her husband. "sandwich?" She asked and lifted one side of her plate up. The kitchen was dimly lit and could have been in any suburban house in America.

"That would be great, please" he continued walking into the kitchen and put his arm around her, kissing her gently on the side of her head. "Drink?" He asked her as he went across to the giant fridge. He took two cans of soda out, retrieved two glasses from the cabinet and filled them both. Sherri finished the presidents sandwich and they walked towards their bedroom for their snack as any other couple would. She knew better than to ask about what had happened and would instead be told when he was ready. Staff were told not to disturb them as they lay down in bed and watched tv as they tucked into their late night snack. The First Lady was a keen lover of British Culture and was busy watching a British Period drama, the President was just happy he could switch off and return to normality, albeit briefly. Sherri had an idea of what had been happening but wasn't briefed on the details. As the President took his notebook out of the side table and picked up his pen from the desk, she guessed what was happening. The President began to pen his speech to the nation as the First Lady chatted to him about the previous episode of the drama…..he needed that, being grounded was incredibly important at a time of high drama.

"My fellow Americans…………I stand before you now not as your President, but as a fellow citizen of this great planet. We face now, an implacable foe, we do so with our friends from around the earth. As you know, we had assembled Armed Forces from across the globe with one intention, to defeat the Voyagers. Several million brave men and women, stretched across the planes of Russia, had a dozen Voyagers in their sites. They were backed up by Navies, Air Forces, Artillery and missile batteries. My fellow Americans, it is my duty to inform you that, as of 20:05 hrs Eastern Standard time, we lost all contact with the three million people under our command. We have checked satellite imagery and we now believe they have been wiped out by the Voyagers. I would normally have waited for families to be informed but we find ourselves in a

situation whereby I need to convey to you the seriousness of the

situation we find ourselves in, as the sacrifices I am going to ask you

to make are both stark and grave........"

He put his pen down, unable to focus on his paper as tears welled up in his eyes. "Sherri, how am I going to do this?" He asked, voice quivering with emotion.

"My dear, nobody ever said being president was an easy task, it's not. You have a responsibility to the people of this Country and beyond to act in their best interests and to do so completely selflessly. Acting in their best interests sometimes means people die, whether that's by sending the military into war, or the Police into danger, that's the job you promised to do. Now I know, the people of America know, you will act in their best interests. What you need to do is......is do what you feel is right, what your heart and your head tell you is right. Do that, and we will pull through and I and your country will be behind you." She wiped a tear away from her eye, leaned forward and kissed the President gently on the top of his head. He smiled at her as she pushed her way back into position on the bed and continued to watch her TV Show.

18

Route five, north Of San Francisco: Debra had stopped for the night in a lay-by and slept in her driver's seat with the seat back as far as it would go. There was little traffic on the small road she had chosen and managed five hours of sleep, in no small part because she hadn't slept for several days before that. Her peace was shattered by a blackbird making scratching noises on the roof of her car as it walked around, investigating the unusual metal creature before it. The sun was slowly rising above the treetops as she surveyed the area in the light for the first time. She wondered whether she should just get her tent out of the trunk and stay there for a few weeks in the hope that everything would blow over but soon discounted that as she remembered the significance of her journey.

Debra went into her trunk and pulled out an old battered metal frying pan, a camping stove and a large shopping bag full of food together with a small stool. She set the stool up next to her car and proceeded to assemble the camping stove. She took a large bottle of water and a pot out of the trunk and set about making some breakfast.

It was peaceful, surrounded by forest which dipped down into a valley in front of her. The sun was now rising fast and she felt the warmth on her skin. She removed two rashers of bacon from a packet, sprayed some of her low calorie oil on the pan and started to fry, adding eggs which she mixed with the bacon. Ten minutes later, she sat back on her stool, bacon and egg sandwich in one hand and fresh coffee in the other. As she squinted into the sun her mind went back to those childhood camping trips again but she couldn't afford to live in her memories for long, she needed to continue her trip north and find Larry. She texted him again, no response.

JPL, Pasadena: "Where is she?" The NASA administrator had contacted Jennifer and passed on what the President had relayed to him, he was keen to talk to Debra given her history with the Voyager Spacecraft, he felt she may be the key to unlocking some of the answers. There was an awkward silence at the end of the phone. Jennifer hadn't seen Debra for at least 24 hours and had no idea where she was having texted her several times with no response.

"I…I don't know sir, I'll find her for you"

"Please do Jennifer, I don't need to explain to you how important this is do I? We need answers for the President and we need them soonest"

"I'll have an answer for you as soon as I can, leave it with me" Jennifer ended the call and grabbed her car keys. She had spent the morning at home packing her belongings. She'd decided that when all this was over she would be retiring and going to her home in Palm Springs to spend her days with her cats, sitting by the pool. Although some would say a little premature, she had decided to pack to get her mind away from the mayhem, it was working well until that call.

Jennifer left her house and walked to her car, locking her door behind her. It was another warm day in California and the birds were forming a chorus at the end of her garden. Jennifer didn't notice them as they were drowned out by sirens in the distance. The madness of the situation had brought out the worst in some

Californians and the wave of violence was coming ever closer. She sat in her car, took a deep breath and drove out of her gates.

At the Jet Propulsion Laboratory she found the team working on the Voyager Spacecraft, but no Debra. She initially swept into the office with all the authority of a women at the very top of her game and then stopped. "Hello......where is Debra?"

Jess unplugged her ear pods and looked across at her. Jennifer was stood in the doorway at the entrance to the office, visibly stressed. The fact that Jess and the team seemed so relaxed did not sit well with her.

"Oh, hey Jennifer, how are things with you?" Jess was not a fluent reader of facial expressions.

"Oh, hey Jess, not good. I've just had the administrator on the phone telling me I have twelve hours to solve this entire mystery and I can't find my god damn team leader! How are you?" Anger transitioned into sarcasm as Jennifer fought hard to control her emotions.

"Wow, ok. Well, she's in Northern California." Jennifer raised her eyebrows in surprise. "She's going to see somebody who she thinks may be able to shine some light on all of this."

Jennifer was impatient "who?"

"Larry, was on the original team when the Voyagers went up" Jennifer's facial expression immediately changed and softened.

"Larry?"

"Yes"

"Larry Manning?"

"Yeah I guess so, he was in charge I think" On hearing this Jennifer walked into the room, pulled a stool from underneath the adjacent desk and sat down. "You look like you need a drink"

"No, no I can't" responded Jennifer as, for a split second, she thought Jess meant an alcoholic beverage. As tempting as it was, this was not the time or place. She soon realised though as Jess nodded towards the coffee machine, "Ah sorry, yes….yes please"

"Are you really ok Jen?" Asked Jess as she walked the few steps to the black, shiny, coffee maker.

"Yeh, I guess" She was relieved that Debra had almost preempted her requirements and gone on her own initiative. Dr Manning was an absolute legend across Astro physics but nobody had spoken to him for years as far as she knew, in fact she wasn't even sure he was still alive given his advancing years. She scanned the room to see what remained of the two Voyager spacecraft in clear glass cases, with dozens of people busy working around them. All of the other work streams within the JPL had been wound down significantly and nearly all resources were now working on the Voyagers. JPL personnel also had unfettered access to any scientific support they needed, from research facilities at the country's finest academic institutions to DNA labs at the FBI and much more. The JPL had become the centre of the storm and it was important that Jennifer retained her calm, she sipped her coffee, stood up and walked around talking to her colleagues in a bid to reassure them she was in control.

New York City, Thursday, 12:00 hrs: "We haven't talked about that feeling since it happened" David was stood next to the bed in their hotel room as he lifted his sweater above his head to put it on.

"I know David, I thought we were going to die, I'm not sure I can talk about it. All I can think about is you and the kids and how I'm not ready to let you all go."

David moved over to the window where Lizzie was looking out across the city, put his arm around her shoulders and looked out at the skyscrapers before them.

"Hey, hey…,it's ok." David attempted to reassure her. "We got plenty of time yet, don't you worry about that."

"I need to see my babies again, it can't be the last time, promise me" she pleaded.

"Listen" reassured David as he hugged Lizzie, kissing the top of her head, "it's not our time honey, it really isn't. Why don't we go back out, it's not good for us to be stuck in here."

"But last time we felt that cold feeling, I know they were near us, I can't feel that again."

"Look we are still here, aren't we? It can't have been them or we'd be gone" She looked up at him. "I mean, it's unlikely it was them and what are the chances it will happen again? Come on, let's go." He tugged at the arm of her sweatshirt and pouted. She smiled back and nodded as she picked up her purse and put her shoes on.

Manchester, England. "Did you hear about Russia?" Dougie was whispering in the back of his carrier with his crew mates. "As I understand it, millions are dead, completely annihilated by the

Voyagers. What chance have we got when they couldn't destroy them with all of that?"

"Dougie, I can hear you, you're beginning to get on my nerves now. All that you've just spouted, did it come from me?"

"No sergeant"

"Well it didn't happen then, from now on if it didn't come from me, it's not real. Do you understand?"

"Yes Sarge…….." suddenly the temperature dropped. "Holy…..did you feel that?" The Sergeant balanced himself with his arms between the two sides of the carrier and as he looked across his soldiers, the colour drained from his face. It was clear he did feel it regardless of what he was about to say. He removed his hands from the tank sharply as if they were on fire, except they weren't, it was the opposite.

"What the f……." Exclaimed Dougie. "Did you feel that?"

"Yes" responded the Sergeant.

"It was them wasn't it?"

"Yes"

"But we are.........well, we're still here" Dougie was as confused as he was relieved.

"Hello zero this is callsign Sierra 11 alpha, are you receiving?" the sergeant was on the radio looking for answers.

"Go ahead 11 alpha" Came the response.

"Did anybody else feel that?"

"Roger that 11 alpha, stand by. All callsigns, radio check, over" one by one all call signs contacted the central call sign to confirm they were still there and all in order. "For information we are putting the drones up to get a full picture" as the sky buzzed from the sound of several drones as they were launched into the air.

Santa Maria Airport, California: Chads Cougar sped past the old USAF F4 Phantom which marked the entrance to the complex. The airport was built by the US Army during the Second World War and, following decades of civil use had recently been returned to the use it was originally designed for. With two runways, the smaller runway was being used to stack four C-5 Galaxys, huge transporter aircraft capable of carrying marines and their vehicles, further aircraft were in the air ready to land as others took off. Chad was at the front of his column of vehicles, they entered the complex and were guided around to the massive planes by airforce personnel. The Military did this kind of thing very well, in the short time the decision had been made to use the airport it had full security including razor wire fixed on top of the fencing, metal hard standing on surrounding land to provide for more space and a team of logistical support units there to provide everything required to airlift the marines in quick time. Chad drove his Cougar at speed, it bounced straight up a ramp under the nose of the giant aircraft, into the heart of the aircraft. There was a sense of complete focus as the Marines quietly went about their business.

The immediate challenge was to just get into the air as the giant C-5 required a minimum takeoff distance which was fractionally longer than the runway. To negate this threat, troops had laid modular aluminium panels behind the start of the runway however this had only taken the runway to just under minimum takeoff length. Given the urgency of the situation, it would have to do. Pilots in the USAF were used to taking risks and there had been significant chatter amongst them in briefings about this particular challenge with some convinced it was going to be their last flight, nevertheless they had no choice and went about their business professionally.

Chad would be on the first plane and was feeling nervous as the ramp was pulled up and the nose lowered, sealing the cargo bay shut. A short time later he felt a jolt as the four General Electric engines sparked into life. Chad got out of his vehicle and made his way to the ladder at the front of the aircraft which leads to the passenger seats. He climbed up and into the only part of the aircraft that looked like a passenger jet, with several rows of seats but no windows, dim artificial lighting contributing to the ambience. Once seated, the 75 personnel were joined by an intelligence officer who stood at the front of the compartment looking across a sea of helmets.

"Ok gentlemen, listen in. This briefing is classified." There was another jolt as the twenty-eight wheels of the aircraft started to roll slowly towards the runway "You are heading for New York City where we have a confirmed siting of Voyagers in Battery Park. For some reason, despite there being plenty of opportunities, they have effectively just basked in the park for several hours. We have plotted their likely path and we believe they are headed towards Newark Energy Centre. Now, I assume you have all been briefed on what happened in Russia?"

There were nods from all as they focused on every word he said.

"The powers that be have said they won't let that happen again and are likely to launch our next offensive using a new strategy. Gents, you are just the contingency for this battle, you will be held back in case the preferred option doesn't work. Once ground assigned you will make your way south to Staten Island, specifically to the Howland Hook Marine Terminal, where you will await further orders. Drivers, you have the co-ordinates. Any questions?" 75 hands shot up in the air. "Any questions not involving what the primary plan is?" 75 hands went back down. "Good, stay safe and look after each other." He went back down the ladder and, when the plane stopped at the end of the runway, he alighted and went on to the next one.

The engines four giant engines fired up to full throttle and the plane began to shake as the pilot released the brakes and it lurched forwards with a mighty roar. As it began to hurtle down the runway the pilot fought with the megalith as it built up speed. He looked at his first officer as both feared it wouldn't be able to lift in the given distance whilst fully loaded. As they closed in on the end of the runway, the plane began to feel lighter and the pilot rotated the flaps on the giant wings, lifting the mighty aircraft into the sky. All on the flight deck breathed a sigh of relief knowing they'd managed a miracle and almost defied science in doing so. The other pilots had been watching as the mighty behemoth took to the sky and breathed a sigh of relief collectively.

In the passenger compartment they were completely oblivious to the miracles taking place around them with their main topic of conversation being what the preferred plan was to destroy the Voyagers.

Downing Street, London: "Prime Minister, worrying news" The Defence Secretary had burst into the Prime Ministers Office whilst disconnecting a call on his mobile phone. The PM was in front of his computer screen looking at maps of reported human loss. He was devastated at the recent losses in Russia and beginning to question his ability to continue in the most senior political appointment in the United Kingdom. He looked up at the Defence Secretary with a furrowed brow.

"Yes?" he was curt, he had lost the will to communicate niceties.

"We have a sighting of Voyagers in the North, just outside Manchester. They appear to be basking, not doing anything in particular. We have military drones up now monitoring them."

The Prime Minister moved his mouse as if to indicate he was finished with his computer, stood up and moved towards a jug of water in the opposite corner of the room. It was a warm day and, even though the window was open, it was still warm in the office with the PM in an unbuttoned lightweight shirt with his sleeves rolled up as opposed to his usual formal business attire. He collected his thoughts as he moved across the room, poured the water, then looked out of the window at the garden and the birds playfully darting between the trees. "I take it we have a precise location?"

"We do, we have them under effective surveillance at the present time, shall we evacuate the surrounding area?"

"What?......no, no not yet. They could move at any time and we will be left to chase our tails around. Let's just bide our time. Don't forget, the next time we attack them will be a full strategic nuclear attack. I don't fancy bloody Armageddon on UK soil any time soon, do you?"

"No, I don't suppose I……" the PM cut across him.

"Let the Americans try this first and if it works, we'll have to consider it but hopefully they will have moved on by then." The PM's popularity had taken a nose dive since the Russia attack and his appetite for risk was not what it was despite there being no effective opposition with all parties drawn together in a war cabinet. "Keep me updated please, and it goes without saying this conversation is between us"

"Of course, listen, I don't blame you. I have family in Manchester and the last thing I want to do is contribute to their downfall. Look, if you don't mind me saying, you look like the pressure is getting to you." The PM shot him a look that would have stopped anybody else in their tracks. "Hear me out, we've known each other a long time and we all need you on the form that won us the last general election by a country mile. What I'm saying is" he began to regret this line of conversation, his voice softened, "what i'm saying is, let's talk. I can see you are bottling things up, spending hours in here on your own. Share the burden, you have an entire cabinet who will happily share your pain."

The PM walked back to his desk, sat in his chair and put his glass of water on a coaster. "You're right, I've closed you all down and I shouldn't have, forgive me." The defence secretary allowed himself a smile. "I'll call a cabinet meeting, and thank you." With that, he opened his journal and took his pen from his top shirt pocket, "I needed that, don't ever be afraid to say what you think." The defence Secretary walked out of the room and left a freshly energised prime minister furiously writing in his journal.

New York: "*leave now, take your possessions and leave the city immediately!*" David and Lizzie were walking through the village having struggled once more to leave the city and were almost taken off their feet by the loud hailer affixed to the police van driving by them. "*Please, leave immediately, your safety cannot be guaranteed if you stay any longer.*" Lizzie looked at her husband, panic in her eyes. They had just walked through Washington Square Park in an attempt to take their minds off what was going on. As they walked through Washington Square Arch, towards 5th Avenue they were remarking how nice it was not to be almost taken off their feet by kids on electric scooters, when the Police vehicle interrupted their daydreaming.

"Honey, we have to go, you know that don't you?" Asked Lizzie

"Of course, we just can't go just yet, I don't want us going from the frying pan and into the fire. I promise you I will get us out of here but we must be patient."

It was clear just from their walk through the Village that the city was emptying gradually and there were still stories of road blocks, looting and car-jacking in the outskirts as people became increasingly more desperate. David was keen to get out too but he was a realist and certainly not a risk taker. His aim was to stall Lizzie until the time was right, then make a break for it and get well away. There was a crackle as the loud hailer sparked into life again,

"Battery Park and surrounding areas is closed, travel south from Canal Street is not permitted. Please make your way North from here."

"Something is happening" whispered Lizzie "I can feel it"

"It's ok, calm down, they're probably just evacuating built up areas systematically. I'm sure it's no more than that."

He lied, he also felt something. There seemed more urgency from the authorities all of a sudden and it hadn't gone unnoticed. This particular Police vehicle was only one of a number, driving down pretty much every street, repeating the same messages.

Northern California: Debra continued to travel North and soon found herself crossing Shasta Lake, towards Mount Shasta. The lake would normally be full of boats and people enjoying the Autumn sunshine. The last time Debra had been to the lake she had been in one of hundreds of cars parked up on the shore before spending the afternoon waterskiing, a very enjoyable afternoon. She thought back to all the other people who joined her that day and wondered where they were now, were they alive?

The sun reflected off the shimmering, still water, now entirely devoid of people. The road was empty too, with the last car Debra had seen probably an hour back, it was clear to her people were now hunkering down having perhaps chosen to move in the early stages of what could only now be described as a world war.

BRRING!!!! BRRING!!!!..........

"Hello?" Debra answered her phone.

"Hi Debs, it's Jennifer"

"Jen, my god I'm so sorry, I forgot to tell you where I was going or what I was doing"

"Don't worry, Jess told me. Look, the President is putting pressure on us to find a solution, I just wanted to say..........well, thank you. You've acted on your own initiative and it goes without saying you have my full support. Does Larry know you're coming?"

"I tried to call him before I left but no answer, god knows what I'll find when I get there. I would have thought Barbara would have answered if Larry couldn't but I just don't know, it's been a while since I had a response to any of my texts to him."

"Will you bring him back here?" Enquired Jennifer, "there are lots of questions and I wonder if he'd like to rejoin the team.....for a period"

"To be honest, if he's up to answering some questions we'll be lucky. It's decades since he retired and has lost contact with everybody but me I think and I don't think that was by accident. Let me see what I find and I'll come back to you. Don't forget, they are in their nineties now." Debra was reluctant to commit to anything or get Jennifer's hopes up.

"Of course, good luck, stay safe and of course, give him my best wishes.."

There was a click as Jennifer ended the call.

Focused back on the task at hand, Debra was enjoying her drive. Peaceful and picturesque, it was something she would often do on her own. As the enormous snow-peaked Mount Shasta came into view, she was again reminded of the power of Mother Nature. Rated as a very high threat of eruption, Debra often thought it had the same potential as Mount St Helens before its eruption in 1980, 'I wonder what the Voyagers would make of that if they were nearby when it happened' she mused as the Road wound through the tree-lined highway.

Ten miles on and she signaled to move off the highway and onto a small side road. The suspension worked hard to soak up the bumps as asphalt turned into a dirt track, throwing a plume of rock and mud behind the back wheels. As the car rumbled along, Debra felt a knot in her stomach as she imagined what she would find when she arrived at Larry's cottage. Would he even be there? If he is, what state will he be in? She began to imagine the worst and was as concerned as she was scared. In a world where human death was now on every corner, Debra had still never seen a dead body and didn't relish somebody she cared about being the first one. As bad, what if he was critically injured? She had no medical training and if she called 911 she was pretty convinced nobody would come.

"At the next exit, please turn right" Debra was snapped out of her daydream by her navigation system. She squinted at the knotted wooden sign which read 'Charlie's Cottage' and smiled, he loved that dog. The even smaller track led through a heavily wooded area and then a clearing around a mile further down. As she drove into the clearing she could see a single-story wooden cottage made of dark oak. There were no other cars in the clearing and no sign of life, the large red door was ajar and the feeling in the pit of her stomach was now overwhelming as she pulled up and activated her parking brake. She opened her car door and stepped out into the warmth of the afternoon. She spluttered slightly as she breathed in

the dirt kicked up by her tyres and she wiped her eyes as they became irritated.

As the dirt cloud cleared away she wiped the dust from her face and walked towards the front door. The house didn't look unkept, but it was also not perfectly maintained, possibly due to the age. There were no flower beds outside so she couldn't tell if anybody had been tending to it. She walked up to the window closest to the door and peered through, nothing. She could see furniture and what looked like a mug on a side table next to the couch, but no real signs of life.

"Larry!!!" Nothing

"Larry!!!" Nothing, just the sound of birds singing and small animals rustling around in the woods around her.

"Barbara……it's Debra…..from the JPL!" nothing.

She had no choice, she'd have to go in. She walked towards the door, clasped the cold metal door handle in her left hand, took a deep breath and.........

The White House: "where exactly?" Enquired the President.

"Near Manchester, in the North West of England. As we understand it, they've only just been found and the British are not looking at evacuations at this point as it's not a residential area, they have forces in the immediate area. There is also a significant power plant within a few miles which is likely to be their target they think." Responded Colonel Miller. After several days very much at the peak of stress, he had now almost relaxed into his new responsibilities, he knew what the President wanted in his updates and, more importantly, what he didn't. The President had also warmed to him and it showed, even occasionally using his first name.

"Wesley, will you tell your counterpart that the United States stands firmly beside them? If we are not successful in New York then they probably already know we are going to have to try the same in the

UK. It's probably why the British Prime Minister hasn't made contact with me yet."

"I will do sir, thank you" with that, the Colonel span around and walked smartly towards the Oval Office door. More relaxed he might be, but you couldn't remove the soldier from him and the President smiled to himself, there was a comfort in that.

The president's Chief of Staff knocked on the Oval Office door and was beckoned in by the president. The president made his way to the two couches and sat on one of them, pointing at the second sofa with his upturned open palm to instruct his trusted friend to join him. He was dressed casually in a shirt with an open collar and smart pants but with no shoes. He had been working pretty much non-stop for days now and had decided that he needed to relax a little more so he could get the best out of himself and those around him.

"Hey Joe. How are you doing?" Enquired the President.

"Forget about me Mr President, how are you? I'm worried my old friend."

The President smiled gently and stood up, put his hands on his hips and puffed his chest out. "You don't have to worry about me, I've never been better" but his body language betrayed his true state. He was stressed both physically and mentally and it was beginning to show. He needed the support of his First Lady and his chief of staff and he realised it. "I've been thinking Joe."

"Go on sir"

"We've had reports of a group of voyagers in Battery Park as you know, what you probably don't know is we now have a group found just outside Manchester in the UK. That means we now know where two of the three groups we are aware of are located. I'm going to call the cabinet together to explain the plan to use strategic nuclear weapons on the voyagers. I have no idea what the reaction will be but we have no choice. I'm going to use executive powers so I don't need agreement but I could sure use it. How do you think they will fall?" The President had sat down again and the two men were now sat opposite each other with their weight forward, only a foot or so apart.

"It's hard to say, I mean, I can't think of an alternative and I'm pretty sure they won't either. I take it General Carter will be in there with us?"

"Yeah, he's a little too keen for my liking......maybe I'm being a little harsh, perhaps he's just very clinical, I wouldn't know what he actually does think."

"Well, in the absence of an alternative and evidence that what we have tried has failed up to this point, I think they'll come around."

"I just wish NASA could give us some kind of idea. I might chase up the administrator before the meeting, if there is any alternative at all I want to take it." He stood up and smiled, put his hand over the top of his chief of staff's clasped hands, turned and walked to his desk.

——

19

Debra pushed the door, it slowly creaked fully open, 'no bad smells' she thought. Not that she knew what smell death brings but it must be bad and the house smelled just fine, a good start. Debra left the door open as she walked further into the house.

"Larry!!" Nothing.

"Barbara!!" Still nothing.

Debra's heart was beating so fast she felt like it was going to burst out of her chest. Although full of old furniture and ornaments that wouldn't look out of place in a museum, there was no dust and the house was clearly well cared for. But where were Larry and Barbara? She didn't have to wait long for the answer.

"Charlie!!!"

"Woof, woof, *grrrrrrrrrr*"

Debra span around to be confronted by a 7 inch tall Dachsund who wasn't happy to see her. As she fixed her gaze on him, the unmistakable figure of Larry loomed into view in the background as he opened the door. He had a look of concern and fear, which soon changed to a beaming smile as he realised who had paid him a visit. He walked into the house, followed by Barbara.

"Debra!! My dear, it's wonderful to see you!!" tears were welling up in his eyes.

"Debra!!" Barbara echoed.

"My god I'm so pleased you're ok" cried Debra as she stepped over the 7 inch wolf and ran into the open arms of Larry. Larry wrapped his arms around her and they cried together for a short time before Barbara had her turn. They were close, more like favourite auntie and uncle than just friends.

"But.......but why did you think something was wrong?" Larry was perplexed.

"I haven't had a response from you for months Larry, I've been worried. And then more recently with the......you know"

"No" he was still confused

"The Voyagers Larry, you must have seen what's been happening"

"Oh yeh, I did. That did take me back, do you remember when we launched those suckers, Debs?" He seemed happy

"Of course, but all the death"

"Well, I stopped watching, to be honest. We live out here and don't really talk to many people so I've just kinda ignored it. I didn't get your messages though, are you sure you sent them to me?"

"Of course I am, I'm not that daft" she smiled warmly at him.

"Come on, you've come a long way, can I make you a coffee? A spot of lunch?" Asked Barbara as she shuffled towards the kitchen.

"You don't have to, I can get it if you like?" responded Debra

"I won't hear of it, you go and make yourself comfortable, and show Larry why his phone isn't working. You're our guest dear." Barbara carried on towards the kitchen and Larry guided Debra towards the living room, the room she had earlier looked at through the window.

As they sat on the sofa, Debra looked at Larry's battered old phone. It still worked, just, but had a cracked screen and had clearly seen better days. She looked at the screen and noticed there was no signal bar, "when was the last time you got a call or message?"

"I don't know, four months I guess?"

"Did you not think that maybe it didn't work anymore?"

"Well, you're the only person we are in touch with and.....well, we just guessed you had a lot on your plate and were too busy to bother with us any more" Larry looked down as he spoke.

"Larry, you and Barbara are two of my favourite people in the world, I love you. Never think I don't have time for you, of course I do. I wish you lived closer and we could see each other a lot more."

Larry smiled and looked back up. Debra picked at the side of his phone and removed the SIM card, wiped it on her sweatshirt, then rubbed it between her thumb and forefinger. As she placed it back into the phone, she smiled back at Larry. "The state of this........have you been playing baseball with it?"

"Haha, it happened a few months ago when we were out with dear little Charlie. I had a stick in one hand and the phone in the other. I got confused and threw the wrong one, I'm just pleased that little Charlie thought it was part of a well rehearsed trick and just sat staring at me with the stick and a confused look on my face."

Debra laughed uncontrollably at the site. Despite these confusing episodes and the fact one of the most brilliant minds she had ever known couldn't even figure out his phone wasn't working properly, she was pleased with how sharp he still seemed, Barbara too. Charlie trotted up a little ramp Larry had built up to the couch and onto a blanket with a gold 'C' embroidered on it, and did several laps before settling down with a contented sigh.

"So, what brings you here, I am guessing this isn't a social visit?" Larry already had half an inkling, but still sought confirmation.

"Well Larry, I know you've been ignoring it, but those Voyagers have caused a lot of problems. They have killed hundreds of millions of people, we are in real trouble" Larry sat back on the sofa.

The Whitehouse: "We've got them!!" Colonel Miller's relaxed state was short-lived "We have them, sir"

"Well come in Colonel" responded the President sarcastically.

"Sorry Mr President" responded the Colonel as he snapped out of his brain fog and remembered whose presence he was in.

"It's ok" smiled the President, "what have we got?"

"Sorry sir, we know where the third pod of voyagers is."

The President had been preparing for the impending cabinet meeting and was hoping for this news before he went in. "Really?" Enquired the President, "where are they?"

"There have been reports of temperature anomalies in Çorlu, Turkey, all afternoon. We are talking 30-degree variations within an hour. There's a small electricity substation just outside the city, probably big enough to supply a few blocks. There were reports of it going dead and when the local Police investigated they reported that all those working in there had disappeared and there was ice on the walls."

"An attack?"

"That's right sir, an attack. They have since been seen basking in a field to the south west of the city."

"Are there any big power stations nearby?" The President was now very interested.

"Well, it's only about 75 miles away from Istanbul, so you can imagine there are substantial power stations in the vicinity."

General Carter was standing with his arms folded next to the presidents desk, looking at the Colonel as he spoke.

"General, I want satellites over there now, this is the third and final pod and we now know where they all are. This could be our best chance."

"Yes, sir" responded the General as he walked past the Colonel and out through the main doors to the office.

As the General left the room, the President called through to his secretary "Can you get the President of Turkey on the line please!"

Northern California: "So you see Larry, everything has been tried and we can't get near them, they just seem to travel at massive speed between cities and destroy and consume everything in sight. Power stations, shopping malls, homes, schools....everything. They leave nothing behind. It's hard to see them coming because you can't see them most of the time, you just feel the temperature change. They've killed hundreds of millions Larry and we are in danger of extinction."

"Power Stations?" Larry was looking at Debra inquisitively, head to one side.

"Power Stations?" Debra wondered where he was going with it.

"You said Power Stations Debs. Tell me, what happens to the power stations?"

"Well, um.......well if you take the first one in New York, the first Power Station attacked. It was emptied, no gas or oil left, no people.....nothing."

"Hmmmm" Larry stood up and straightened his slacks before making his way towards the kitchen. "I'm gonna get myself an iced tea, want one?"

Debra was staring at him, wondering if he heard her response "uh, yeah I guess"

"I don't drink much coffee any more, doesn't agree with me. Shall we see what Barbara is fixing up? She makes the best Reuben sandwiches, if we're lucky that's what she's making." He smiled.

Little Charlie was immediately alerted to their movement and his head rose sharply from his little bed. He stared intently with one ear folded back and left jowl stuck above his large canine tooth. This was serious; a stranger in his house was in danger of moving out of his field of vision. He stood up and ran down the ramp, anticipating they were going to the kitchen his legs worked overtime to get him there first. Once in the doorway, he monitored them both as they walked towards where Barbara was indeed serving up her famous Rueben.

"You do eat meat I take it my dear? You're not a vegetarian now are you?"

"No Larry, no I'm not" Debra smiled back as they walked past Charlie and into the kitchen. He followed on looking up at them as he trotted along.

"NASA have been asked for solutions Larry, they're fast running out of ideas. I was already coming to see you to ask but if I hadn't I suspect I would have been told to. Larry……..Larry" Larry was staring out of the window as Charlie growled in the corner.

"You'll be lucky to get too much sense out of him Debs, he had a stroke a few years ago. Not a bad one and he's pretty much recovered now, but it was enough to slow him down. From time to time this happens and he just stares blankly for a while. Don't worry, he'll be back in the room before you know it. Little Charlie seems to know when it's going to happen and let's me know, he's such a good boy."

"Debra! What are you doing here?" Exclaimed Larry with a beaming smile on his face. "I haven't seen you in years, it's so lovely!"

"Darling, you've had one of your funny turns" Barbara was talking gently to him, as if to do otherwise would upset him. She was running her hand through his scruffy grey hair. Larry looked confused.

"Hey Larry, it's ok, I understand" Debra felt she should say something and it was all she could think to say. "Let's have these lovely Reuben's Barbara has made, they look awesome!"

Larry smiled and hugged his wife. Debra didn't know what to feel. She felt let down that they hadn't shared his illness with her yet understood why they wouldn't want to worry her, especially as it was relatively minor. She felt relieved that her worst fears hadn't been realised and they were both safe and relatively well. Then there was the overriding feeling, fear. Despite trying to tell herself not to, Debra had built up her hopes that Larry was the key to solving the mystery. She wasn't sure how much longer mankind had left given the mass killings in such a short period of time and, if anybody was capable of thinking their way out of it, Larry was. She could feel a chance to solve the mystery slipping out of her grasp.

As Debra pondered the position she now found herself in, Barbara finished up the Reuben's and Larry made the iced tea, "fresh lemon?" He cheerfully enquired, seemingly oblivious to his earlier turn.

"Sure, why not" she smiled. Debra then put the food and drink on a tray to be taken in.

"I'll take it Barbara" Debra took the tray and walked with it into the living room, closely observed by Charlie.

JFK Airport: The giant military aircraft floated towards the runway, tiny lights twinkling to guide the giant flying machines in. A short screech marked the conclusion of the plane's descent as it hit the tarmac and the huge jet engines were thrown into reverse, sucking in thousands of litres of moist New York air. Up in the passenger compartment, the 75 men of the United States Marine Corps were standing up ready to alight the aircraft. Chad had spent most of the flight napping, dreaming about his wife back home, going on vacation to Hawaii. He unfastened his seatbelt and pushed the jacket he'd been using as a makeshift blanket, from his shoulders.

"Guys, we're going into a hot zone now, don't take anything for granted. We will be guided to one of the runways which is being left empty so we can form up. Once all flights have deposited our men and vehicles we will leave as one. You need to be switched on and sharp!!" The Lieutenant stood at the front of the passenger compartment and had the men's full attention. "If anything goes wrong out there we stick together, is that understood?"

"YES SIR!" They responded as one.

"No first-class lounge?" Whispered Chad......nobody heard. They filed down the ladder and onto the cargo deck where they got back into their vehicles. Red lights began to flash as the massive rear ramp began to lower and cracks of sunlight streamed into the aircraft. As the ramp hit the tarmac, Chads Cougar sped onto the runway together with the other vehicles and were guided to the empty runway to await their fellow Marines.

Northern California: "We lost millions in that attack apparently......we haven't managed to lay one finger on them yet." Explained Debra.

"What do they look like?" Enquired Larry.

"Well, they're tall, real tall. When you can see them they are mainly black with red...."

"No Debs, the Voyagers, what do they look like now? They must have flown billions of miles in a matter of hours, how did they not break up? I'd love to see them"

Debra took her phone out of her back pocket and went into her photo app. She shuffled herself closer to Larry on the sofa and turned her phone so it was on its side. Larry lowered his spectacles from his forehead and squinted as he looked at each photograph. Debra watched his face as a single tear rolled down his cheek. He was looking at his proudest achievement, his life's work. Once she had got to the last photo, she turned her phone back around and pressed the button on the side, turning the screen dark again. As she shuffled forward to place it in her back pocket she saw Larry shuffle forward and she held her hand up to aid him in standing up.

"You ok Larry?"

Charlie was on full alert.

"I'm fine" he shuffled towards a large sideboard and tugged at one of the draws as it creaked, opening wide. Larry reached inside and pulled out a dark red tin, closed the drawer again and walked back to the sofa.

"Wow, what's that?" Asked Debra.

Larry sat down next to her silently, a second tear now rolling down his weathered face. Barbara and Charlie were also now watching intently from the chair opposite as he brushed some dust off the top of the box. He slowly opened it with both hands and sighed as he looked inside.

The White House: "Thank you for coming with such short notice, this is the first full cabinet meeting for a day or so and that's my fault. Things have been moving so quickly I've spoken to you individually, we're a team and I should do better. I apologise."

The cabinet room was packed full of the President's government, most of whom were pleased to be back in play. There had been talk the President was feeling the pressure and they felt he should be not only sharing the burden, but the executive decision making.

"Colonel Miller will take you through the current situation as we know it." He glanced over and nodded towards his intelligence colonel who was standing near the door.

"Studies of the Voyager's DNA have identified around 36 unique creatures so far. They appear to be split into three 'pods' and we've been able to track how they've moved across the planet from when they arrived. The three pods, after killing hundreds of millions, appear to now be settled in three areas. The first place is just outside Manchester in the United Kingdom. They appear to be basking there and are under surveillance using drones and satellites. We are in contact with the British Prime Minister and they have a significant buildup of forces in the area, we are helping provide air cover from our bases in the UK." The Colonel stepped forward to the table and poured himself a glass of water, then sipped from it, placing it back down on a Whitehouse-branded coaster.

"The second pod are outside the city of Çorlu in Turkey, about 75 miles from Istanbul. Again, there are significant forces built up in the area and significant surveillance. The final pod are in Battery Park, New York City" There was an audible gasp from some of the government who hadn't been briefed. "They have been there for some time. We have done our best to evacuate the city and push the population up towards northern Manhattan without getting too close to them."

"Thank you, Colonel. So, that's where we are, we know where they are and they seem to have slowed down for some reason. They have been pretty much visible since they moved to their current position, we don't yet know why. The scientists have two theories; one, that they have effectively overfed and now need to rest, similar to how we'd feel if we'd over eaten and two, that they haven't eaten enough, they need more and are basking to build up energy. They are within striking distance of large power stations in all three locations, it is a reasonable theory that is where they are headed. Now, you have all been briefed on what happened in Russia?" There were nods around the room. "Well, we can't have a repeat, throwing our military into the slaughter knowing we are likely to fail. We have to do something different and analyse what we haven't tried. We have tried conventional weapons, that hasn't worked, we've tried…..well the Russians have tried small yield tactical nuclear weapons, that didn't work. I can only see one more option."

In the corner of the room, the secretary of the interior was slowly shaking her head, strongly suspecting what would come next….she was right. "Large scale, high yield strategic nuclear weapons. I have spoken to other world leaders and we have agreed on the pathway forward. There will be a strike on the Voyagers currently in Battery Park using weapons from us, the Russians and the British."

"No……you, you can't!" Shouted Henry Parker, the Secretary of Education, banging his fist on the desk as he did so. Conversation erupted around the room…..

"I can Henry, and I will, with or without your support." The room was stunned into silence, they knew he was right.

Northern California: Debra, Barbara and Charlie were all staring intently at Larry as he pulled a small metal disc from the box. Debra was a little disappointed when she realised what it was.

"I was given this as a memento, it's the third gold disc." They gasped, he continued "The first two were much bigger and went on the Voyager spacecraft, the third was much smaller and presented to me." He was smiling from ear to ear as he fumbled further into the box, a few moments later he removed his hand, clutching a scrap of paper. "I found it" he announced triumphantly, "I knew it was in here somewhere." He placed the box on the small table next to the sofa and focused intently on the scrap of paper before straightening it out on his thigh. He picked it up and cleared his throat, looking across to Debra.

"My dear, I don't think I can help you, I know how disappointing that must be."

Debra was visually deflated, breathed a long sigh and sat back on the sofa.

"But, I did see this coming, or something like it." He passed the scrap of paper to Debra, as she touched it she was surprised by just how fresh it felt given its age. It was a letter addressed to Larry, from the NASA Administrator and was sent during the period he spent as a College Professor whilst in his thirties:

Dear Professor Manning,

Thank you for your letter dated 3rd April 1967, I have taken the liberty of sharing the contents with some of my team at NASA. In your letter, you point out your concerns regarding the increased intensity of our attempts to make contact with life from other worlds. You assert that in doing so we risk making far more powerful and intelligent beings aware of our location and the resources we may possess. Whilst we don't agree with your assertion, we are very interested in your theories on interstellar space travel and power inversion....

"Where's the rest of the letter?" asked Debra as the ripped page brought her to a grinding halt.

"I honestly don't remember. Shortly after that, I returned to NASA and then the Jet Propulsion Laboratory. You see the Administrator at the time was keen on mavericks and that's what I was seen as. They gave me the disc as it was ironic, give the guy who thought trying to make contact with ET was a bad thing, a replica of the gold discs meant to educate and inform them."

"So what was your theory?" Asked Debra with a degree of urgency.

"I can't remember Debs, I'd hoped that I would remember once I saw the letter but it's not helped at all." With that, Larry sat back and started to breathe a little heavier.

"I think he needs a little nap now Debra, let's give him an hour, we can go out back with Charlie and relax. He'll be much better when he wakes again."

Barbara stood up as Larry's heavy breathing soon became snoring and grabbed the blanket draped around the back of her chair. She gently placed it around her loving husband and signalled for Debra to follow her out of the room so they could leave Larry in peace. Charlie spent his life learning to anticipate what was coming next and had already zipped down his little ramp and was waiting for them in the doorway to the kitchen.

20

Istanbul, Turkey: the attack sirens started whaling again, Voyagers had been spotted by a drone operator, basking in the mid-afternoon sun in a disused open quarry to the northwest of the city. This had now become a frequent occurrence, a large-scale attack followed by a siting of Voyagers resting before the next move. Turkish and nearby Bulgarian Army Units were mobilised, moving towards the North of the City from the East and West flanks.

The sirens were almost counterintuitive as they appeared to have the effect of panicking their own population whilst warning the Voyagers that something was afoot. For now, though, they continued to bask and seemed almost relaxed as the evening moved into the night. But appearances can be deceiving and this wasn't the case, the Voyagers were in need of another feed as they used an inordinate amount of fuel just to keep going and this particular pack hadn't fed for some time. They weren't relaxed, they were exhausted, hungry and this made them very, very dangerous.

Üsteğmen (equivalent rank to Lt) Ahmet Avci sat in his modernised Leopard 2 main battle tank, awaiting further orders from senior officers. His unit had been on the move most of the day and it was looking like it would be a long deployment. "I can hear you, you know" he said to the young soldiers in his command, "and if I can hear you so might they, keep your discipline".

Ahmet was a family man with young children and often thought young children defined both his work and home life, given the young age of his tank crew.

"Sorry sir, it's just been a long day and I think we could do with a break, it's hard to concentrate" retorted Deniz, the youngest and most confident of his troops.

Some people occasionally straddle the line between confidence and arrogance, Deniz was squatting on it. A charismatic character he often made some great points, but sold them badly.

"Just be quiet Deniz, I do not speak for you to respond, it's an instruction dressed as a request" he smiled and Deniz realised now wasn't the time to answer back.

It was still hot in the tank and the four men were grateful for the fresh air coming in through the main crew hatch. Ahmet glanced down at his watch and imagined his wife and children preparing for their evening meals back home.

"Sir?"

"What Deniz, you are really trying my patience now"

"I need to go to the bathroom"

"You have been put on this earth to test me......go outside" As Deniz made his way out of the tank, Ahmet started writing in his notepad. Deniz made his way to a small bush out of the public gaze and then slowly dawdled back to the tank.

Istanbul's infrastructure had struggled to keep up with its nearly 16 million population. Power cuts were relatively common and often planned in by electricity companies in order to carry out much-needed maintenance, with notice given. From time to time there would be a complete power cut. Several power stations feed the mega city and are dotted on the outskirts, powered by several sources including natural gas and coal. The Voyagers didn't seem close to any of them but it was clear they were their target. Turkish forces had been deployed around the power plants for some days in a vain hope they could deter or stop any attack.

"Yes sir" Ahmet responded on the radio as Deniz got back into the vehicle. "OK guys, we have been given orders to move to within one kilometre of the voyagers, this is going to be very risky so switch on." He instructed his soldiers, tapping the side of his helmet with his left index finger, he was looking at Deniz as he said it.

With that, the driver started the giant 1500 horsepower diesel engine and the tank lurched forward, joined by several dozen other tanks across both flanks. Turkish military commanders watched drone footage from above as small plumes of dirt made their way closer to the quarry. There was an air of inevitability in the air as the drone cameras focused on the still-basking voyagers in the quarry. The tanks circled the quarry at around a one-kilometre distance. Orders had been given to fire on the voyagers once in position. This was a contingency in case Generals were taken out of the game through an attack.

All of a sudden.........

PHT!!

There was a complete power blackout! The power cut covered the entire city of Istanbul, the metropolitan area beyond and the surrounding towns and cities. Nothing was working, everything from traffic lights to office blocks, all internet connections were down, mobile phone masts.....nothing. Generals could no longer monitor the action or give any orders, they were in complete darkness.

Whilst the vehicles could no longer communicate with commanders, they could still coordinate with each other due to the fact their electricity was provided through batteries in their tanks. Individual tank commanders soon realised there was no longer communication back with HQ. They talked amongst themselves and decided Ahmet would give the command. Their engines were off and for a split second, the sound of birds was all that could be heard.

Deniz's heart was in his mouth, this was the first action he'd experienced in his relatively short life. Without saying anything, Ahmet put his hand on Deniz's left shoulder, looked down at him......

"Ready?" Deniz looked up at him, peeking out from underneath his helmet, beads of sweat slowly meandering down his forehead. He looked like a scared child. Deniz nodded.

"On my command, open fire" Ahmet shouted down the radio, his right hand raised in the air. "3, 2, 1……..fire!!!" Flames leapt out of the turrets of dozens of the most modern battle tanks with a thunderous roar, seconds later they smashed into the quarry, completely obliterating it. Barrage after barrage as subsequent shots were fired.

And then...........nothing.

But this time it was different, no ice cold chill, no complete annihilation of the human attackers......nothing.

Ahmet looked down at Deniz, who looked back under his helmet. He held the radio mic' to his mouth "Can I have a sit' rep' from all callsigns please?" One by one the other tank commanders responded, and it would appear there had been no casualties. "We are going to move forward with callsign O21B into the quarry and check, provide cover." The tank jolted forward once more, towards the quarry. There was complete silence in Ahmet's tank, none of the men thought this was the end and knew they needed to remain focused. The two tanks moved towards the massive plume of smoke which marked the landing point of of their combined ordinance. As they moved over the lip of the quarry, they couldn't really see what was inside due to the dust that had been kicked up. The two tanks stopped a few hundred meters short of the last place the voyagers had been seen.

"Deniz, you're with me" instructed Ahmet as he threw open the hatch, letting in a dusty ray of light, and climbed out of the tank. There was a pungent smell of nitroglycerin, sawdust, and graphite swirling in the air as they got closer to the site. Deniz followed him out as Ahmet landed on the dusty quarry floor. Deniz joined him and they walked slowly towards the dust cloud, as the air cleared they could hardly believe what they could see. Twelve giant bodies, black and red, not moving. They got closer and stopped just short, Deniz picked up a piece of wood from the ground and prodded one of the corpses, nothing. They were dead. Always one to let himself down he sniffed the stick and received a slap around the back of his head from Ahmet.

Back at HQ in Istanbul, the power switched back on. They had no idea what had happened. As the screens flickered back to life the drone beamed back footage of the dead voyagers in the quarry to be greeted by cheers at HQ. This was the first victory against the Voyagers and it had been achieved despite a power cut. The human race needed this win!

News soon reached the major governments of the world but celebration was muted. Casualties were approaching apocalyptic levels and if this was the likely ratio of losses there wasn't long left.

The Turkish government agreed with the United States and other nations that the bodies of the voyagers would go to several facilities around the world to undergo a thorough dissection and examination.

The White House: "All of them?"

"Yes Mr President"

"No casualties?"

"None sir"

"Send a message to the Turkish government from the people of America, thanking them for their bravery"

"Yes sir" message passed, and the president's PA scuttled off as the throng of senior military advisors closed around.

The President looked around the room, a hint of a smile on his face finally. "This changes nothing" he declared. "We now need to double down and annihilate what's left. The remaining voyagers may now be even more dangerous if they know about what has happened in Turkey, we can't risk them going on a rampage. What's the eta for the full attack in New York?"

"Still a few hours Mr President, we are waiting for the all-clear, the point at which we have made best attempts to get people away. It's also important the wind is moving the right way, we don't want fallout hitting other major population centres."

The president sat back down on the sofa in the Oval Office and furrowed his brow. It was the first piece of good news in a long time but he had a thirst for answers that couldn't be quenched. "How long will it take to get answers on what they are, I mean physically?"

"We are sending scientists out to study them, as are the British and Japanese, we will get answers as soon as possible but it's probably going to take a few days at the very least. A few days of scientists working around the clock and catching a few breaks" responded the chief of staff.

Northern California: Larry had awoken from his nap and was sipping another fresh iced tea. "My dear, have you ever wondered why? Why them and why now? What attracted them here? When you find the answer to that question, you will surely find the key to saving humanity" And with that he returned to sleep, dreaming of his happy place, with his wife and little Charlie in their picture-perfect cottage in Maine. Debra kissed him gently on the forehead, hugged Barbara as she walked past and then left through the main door.

A stream of sunlight through the trees dilated her pupils as she entered the outside world again and the stale smell of the house was immediately forgotten. As her thumb rested on the unlock button of her car key she reflected on the few words Larry had managed whilst she was in there. Why? What? A gentle smile crossed her face as she reflected that, despite his advancing years, apparent fragility and need for 23 1/2 hours of sleep per day, he was still as sharp as he was in 1977.

She got into her car and began the drive back, she decided not to put the radio on as the ongoing disaster would be the only theme. More dead, more injured, more destruction and no answers. In this almost empty part of California, among the forests and wildlife, you could be forgiven for thinking the last few weeks hadn't happened and that's what she wanted to think, for a while at least.

The Road meandered through the forest. There were no other cars on the road and she sat in silence as she drove. She started to reflect again……..why now? What was it that triggered this deadly encounter? She pulled the car into a lay-by. Why are there none here? She got out of her car, shut the door and listened as the birds sang. Twigs cracked in the background and bushes rustled as the small creatures of the forest went about their business seemingly unaware of the disaster unfolding only a few hundred miles away. Why?

After five minutes of watching and listening Debra returned to the old Buick she had owned for over 20 years, put the key in the ignition but didn't turn it.........why? Why did Voyager 1 return to the centre of New York? Why did Voyager 2 go to the centre of Tokyo? Why?

Why?....... Debra seemed lost in her own thoughts. She then turned the key in the ignition and the car made a groan as it failed to spark. She turned it again and the same happened......"Not now!!!!" She popped the hood and went around to look at the engine. Despite her intelligence and understanding of spacecraft, Debra had never even tried to fix a car before. She knew the basics of mechanical engineering but had no idea how to fix this. She looked at the engine and whispered to herself "Come on Debra, you have sent spacecraft 15 billion miles across space, you can sort this out. It's just about energy.........I need to create a spark to turn the parts in the engine to create energy. Energy is the key" She stepped back, mouth open, and took a deep breath.......... "Energy is the key," she said again as her eyes raised upwards.

BRING......BRING

Debra was awoken from her trance. She looked at her phone to see the name of her beleaguered boss.

"Hi Jen" she had guessed Jennifer was phoning for an update.

"Hey Debra, I have an update for you" Debra was confused, she hadn't expected that, and Jennifer sounded almost chirpy.

"Go on" Debra responded.

"There has been an attack"

"Oh no!!" Responded Debra….was she too late?

"No, no, it's good news. We've killed a pod of Voyagers, well the Turkish and Bulgarian Militaries have. It's great news." Jennifer sounded very excited.

"Wow, I wasn't expecting that, but how?" Quizzed Debra.

"To be honest, we don't know but the bodies are going to be studied, this could be it Debs."

"Wow, ok, well that does sound like amazing news. Where will they go?"

"They are not going anywhere at the moment, that's deemed both too much of a risk and too slow, so scientists are being sent out to them so we can study them quick time. We are so lucky though, it nearly went horribly wrong." Reflected Jennifer.

"How so?"

"Well, there was a complete power cut just before the military opened fire. Nothing working, no internet, no lights, no electricity.....nothing. No idea how the military commanders managed to communicate, so very lucky." Responded Jennifer.

"Huh, would you believe it? That does sound lucky, could have gone very wrong." Said Debra, thinking about what she had just heard.

"Oh, I do have an update from Larry but probably not the panacea we all hoped it would be, I'll catch you when I get back. My batteries running low so I'd better go" Debra was not being entirely honest, her phone was plugged into the car and almost fully charged.

"Ok hun, speak to you soon, drive safely," she said as she disconnected the call.

As the conversation ended, Debra began to reflect on the conversation she'd just had and the conversations she had with Larry. 'Energy is the key' she repeated to herself as she got back into her car and sat back into her black leather driver's seat. She now seemed almost as if she were in a trance........ 'energy' She wasn't paying any attention at all as she once again turned the ignition key and..........

It started!!!

Debra awoke from her daydream and gasped, put the car into drive and started to pull back onto the road. As the car reached cruising speed her mind drifted yet again. Energy; did the voyagers draw energy from the spacecraft? "But the spacecraft have hardly any energy left. How does that help them and how did they find earth?" She reasoned out loud. She remembered when they processed the picture Voyager took back in 1990 which showed a picture with the earth a tiny blue dot, how did they find us? She carried on thinking and theorising all the way back to the lab.

By the time she'd returned to the lab, Debra had theorised exactly what the Voyagers were doing and why. But it was only a theory and she needed to not only test it, but find somebody brave enough to allow her to do it. She ran straight into the lab where she found the rest of the team in various states of work. They looked at her as she entered the room.

"Well?" Questioned Gus expectedly, "Did he say anything?"

"Very little" said Debra, "but so much".

Gus tilted his head, he'd never understood nuance and the stress certainly hadn't improved his understanding.

"He said we need to understand why, why they are here and why now. That's all he said but it got me thinking. Then the strangest thing happened. My car broke down."

"Well that's not strange" quipped Gus, "I've been telling you that will happen for months" Although not a mechanic, he had been telling Debra that the engine wasn't supposed to rattle and steam that much for months now but she had ignored him, reasoning that her journey to work was so short that, even if she broke down, it wouldn't be a major issue for her.

"No, no that's not the strange thing, it's the way it got me thinking. The Voyagers found our spacecraft right?" They nodded. "When we examined Voyager 2, what was missing? The gold record, with a helpful map of our solar system, and the Uranium 238 plate. They did exactly what we wanted, they read the map and then used the uranium to understand how far or long they needed to travel. So that's the how, the easy bit to a certain extent. Why now? Look at this map."

They all shuffled over to the large QLED screen with a map displayed. Debra started inputting data into the computer linked to the screen. It showed where the known attacks had occurred and where there was no site of the Voyagers. She then layered on top of that where the attacks had been most intense, together with the only known occasion they left without annihilating everything they came into contact with.

"So what do these all have in common?" Asked Debra.

"Big cities?" Responded Jess, "Not really a surprise given that's where most of our forces had built up."

"You're right Jess, but there's something else that separates New York, for example, and rural Russia. Energy. The amount of energy it takes to keep a city like New York going is phenomenal the amount needed for a village in Russia is significantly less."

"Obviously," remarked Gus

"Look at the one place where there was success. Istanbul in Turkey, they attacked and there was a total power cut at the same time. Complete power cut, nothing worked at all for miles around. What happened? They stopped, it was like they were blind. Compare that with when we have used nuclear weapons, it's made them even stronger and more aggressive."

"So it's the energy they want?" Asked Jess

"It's more than that. They don't just want it they need it, they need it to see us, it's how they smell and it's what they eat. When it goes they can't survive and have to go. They are basically harvesting us for energy. The only way to stop them is to stop using energy, cut the power completely."

"You mean they're not here to annihilate us, we're just getting in their way?" Asked Gus.

"That and we are competition for resources that they need."
Responded Debra.

"It's a great theory," said Brian, who had been uncharacteristically quiet up to this point. "So you are saying that the most effective enemy to fight the Voyagers, is nothing? Literally nothing at all, we just stand there and do nothing?" By now he was animated and gesticulating towards the map.

"I haven't finished. They dispose of humans because we are also using the energy and their need is so great, they need sole use. Can't you see? They're not fighting us because they're aggressive, they're fighting us because they're desperate. We saw what happened in Istanbul. Carcasses piled up outside the city as voyagers couldn't function."

Brian's facial expression changed as he thought through what she was saying.

"You know what the rumours are, don't you? They are going to use the big nukes to take them out." Jess said, eyes wide as she spoke.

"Listen, let's say you are right Debra, and let's say you are too Jess." Brian was becoming more accepting of Debra's theory, hearing what the alternative may look like. "How on earth are we going to get that information to the people that need it." It was a good question, Debra needed to move fast.

"Good point, I need to speak to Jen, the President needs to hear this." Said Debra as she stood up and reached into her back pocket for her phone.

22

New York City: David and Lizzy were walking along Park Avenue as a column of tanks drove past in the opposite direction. As they got to the corner of 54th street their phones omitted a loud alarm sound, signifying an emergency alert message.

......this is an emergency message from the United States Government.....those not already looking to leave New York City must do so immediately......New York City is under the imminent threat of attack......if you are not at home do not return and leave immediately.......

They looked at each other. It was the first message either had received for a couple of days as the mobile signal had flat-lined following the attacks. Both had thought it was a message from Ethan and Emily who they hoped were now safely with David's parents in Nebraska.

"What?!" Exclaimed Lizzy, crying and coughing simultaneously.

"Don't panic, I need to think" responded David.

The Whitehouse, Washington DC, 18:00 hrs: "Mr President, General Carter is on the line, sir". The President's secretary had patched through to the President's desk in the Oval Office. The President had been busy looking through briefing papers on the impact of nuclear fallout.

"Put him through" President Williams responded. His secretary informed the General he was about to speak to the president. President Williams picked up the phone.

"Michael, the warning has gone out. Please tell me there is an alternative." The president was almost pleading with the senior military man.

"I wish there was sir, we don't have long left. We are pulling all our forces out of the New York area at the moment and there should be a complete evacuation within the next two hours." The General sounded almost cold as if he was on automatic pilot.

"Not a complete evacuation General, there's still millions of civilians in the City!!" barked the President. He wanted to remind the General of what was at risk.

"Sorry sir, we are doing our best." His voice softened.

"Well, I've spoken with President Subinski in Russia and Prime Minister Richard's in the UK. We will coordinate multiple attacks using nuclear weapons from the Western Seaboard with our own weapons, Russian ICBMs launched West from Eastern Russia and from British Trident Submarines in the Atlantic. By attacking from multiple directions we are hoping that it decreases the opportunity for Voyagers to intercept them. I want to give civilians the best chance of getting out so the attack will commence in 4 hours at 10 pm. The voyagers seem to attack once the sun has set and it's setting at around 9 pm and this gives us our best chance to maximise the impact." The President was effectively relaying General Carter's own plan back to him as if he didn't know what it entailed. The General found this reassuring as it was clearly understood by those in the chain of Command.

"Sir, this the only option, you're doing the right thing" General Carter reassured the President.

"I hope so Michael, I really hope so. I have set DEFCON 1, we haven't been here before, I had hoped we never would."

Pasadena "So let's say you're right, how on earth do we get this to the powers that be?" Brian asked for a second time, Debra seemed to have drifted off.

"The administrator, you know he has a direct line to the President. Convince him and we can convince the President. This could be our only chance, Brian, the attacks could start again at any time across Europe and America!" Responded Debra.

In the background, the news was playing on a rolling loop. A reporter could be seen in front of a mosque which was burning in the dark of night, society was breaking down. Debra grabbed her phone again and looked through her contacts. The NASA administrator had given her his number should she need it and she thought, well, she couldn't think of a circumstance more needy than this. She dialed his number and to her amazement, he picked up almost immediately.

"What's up?" He was short.

"Sir, I have a theory that you need to hear. I think the more we throw at these voyagers the stronger they'll get. I think it's the energy, be that oil, gas, electricity or god forbid, nuclear, that's giving them strength, in fact, I think it's why they're here." She paused for breath. "Look at the solitary victory we have had so far. They were celebrating us achieving the victory in Istanbul despite the power cuts but I think it's why we achieved it. It's the only difference between that and every loss we have incurred. We need to cut the juice sir, turn everything off and see if that stops them. I think it will weaken them" She stopped talking, hoping for a positive response.

"So, Debra, your genius idea is to do nothing......I mean literally nothing? Just switch the lights out and hope they just toddle off. Are you serious?" He sounded dismissive but he wasn't, he was testing her resolve. This was something he was going to have to pass on to the President and if she didn't believe it, the President certainly wouldn't.

"I know it sounds far-fetched but we have cranked this up bit by bit and don't have much further to go. Every time we've done that, they've become stronger and more powerful. The only time that's not happened is in Istanbul, in Istanbul everything switched off and they were left vulnerable to attack. Please sir, we need to get this to the President, the rumour is the next thing we try is a large-scale nuclear attack. If i'm right, that will give them even more power and strength. You can stop this." She sounded desperate and was. Having thought this through for some time now she was absolutely convinced a full-scale nuclear attack would be the beginning of the end.

There was silence on the other end of the phone as the administrator not only digested this theory but realised he would have to explain this, and then sell it to the President.

"Very well, I'll pass this on. We are desperate and I'm willing to try anything, let's hope he is as benevolent." With that, he put the phone down and Debra was left to ponder as to whether he would really speak to him and what his response would be if he did.

The Whitehouse, Washington DC: "Sir, we are ready to go. I understand that New York is pretty much as empty as we can get it. The alert system seems to have done the trick and estimates are that the city is pretty much empty with only a few hundred thousand left there, mainly those who are too old, disabled or stubborn to move. The Voyagers are still in Battery Park, they haven't moved for several hours and we have a live link watching them." General Carter had sensed a deep reluctance in the president's voice the last time they spoke so had decided to make the trip across the city from the Pentagon to the Whitehouse to reassure him.

The president was watching a small robin on the Whitehouse lawn, pecking gently at the soil, looking for a tasty treat. He was captivated by how the robin could detect where his dinner was with almost total accuracy. Bach's Cello Suite Number One was playing quietly in the background. The President felt this was the perfect music for the Oval Office as it drew the smokiness out of the wood panelling, perfectly augmenting the historic atmosphere. He was doing everything he could to relax, believing that it would engender more focused thinking and clearer decision-making.

"General" he turned around and moved his spectacles from his forehead, over his nose, he focused….."General, the way you talk concerns me." He was stern.

"Sir?" The General was clearly confused.

"You talk about the most vulnerable members of our society like they are expendable. That's why you will never be a politician and I will never be a military general." His voice had softened slightly.

"Sir, I don't under…"

The President didn't give him time to finish his sentence as he cut across him "Don't worry, you don't have to." The president was pensive as he looked around the room before fixing his gaze on those pictures of the past presidents again, his inspiration.

"Sir, we need to act now. There are two groups of voyagers left, half of those are in Central Park. We act now and we wipe out half of what's left! Sir……" he sounded almost desperate.

"Is there no other way?" The President had a nagging feeling the General was desperate for his last hoorah before retirement.

"No sir, there's not" The General was now getting frustrated and it showed. "I need your order, sir, I need it now"

"OK General, you……"

"Sir!!" The door to the Oval Office swung open dramatically to reveal the president's Secretary armed with the encrypted phone. "Sir, it's the NASA administrator, he says it's urgent!" A usually calm women, her excitement made the President sit up and take notice.

"Was that a yes, sir?" the General interrupted, desperate for his answer.

"Stand by, General, two minutes will make no difference will it?" He was curt again.

"No" responded the general despondently.

The President took the phone from his secretary, "This had better be good….." the president said to the administrator.

"Sir, thank you for taking my call"

"Cut the niceties, we don't have time. Have you got me an update?" This crisis had turned the President into a more focused and demanding character, some said it made him seem like a more credible leader than ever.

"Yes sir" the administrator was slightly flustered, "one of my staff has a theory around this but she's not just any member of staff, her name is Debra Johnson."

Silence.

"Sorry sir, there's no reason you would know who she is but she was one of the original scientists on Voyager 1 back in 1977. She really understands the machines and has been working on them ever since."

"Ok Bill, let's hear it then, what's she got?" The President had softened again.

"Well, she has spoken to the original Voyager lead scientist, Dr Larry Manning. Following the conversation she has theorised that the Voyagers are desperately searching for energy, almost like scavengers, and that humans are just competition for what they see as food."

The administrator went on to explain Debra's theory in detail with the president interrupting to clarify and question him. He put the phone down and looked at the General. General Carter had gotten the general gist of the conversation and didn't like where it was going.

"Sir, are you suggesting we do nothing? Against the greatest threat to mankind, we just lay down our arms and do nothing?" He was perplexed and beginning to think the President was losing touch with his sanity.

"No General, what I'm saying is we do exactly what we did in Istanbul, but this time on purpose. Listen, your plan…..our plan until now, would have us destroy New York City, make it uninhabitable and kill some of our most vulnerable citizens. Whilst I'm not 100% sold on this theory, I think we give it a go, it certainly seems more logical than our alternative. Gena (the President's Secretary), I need you to get the cabinet together, this will need to be well coordinated. Trying to get everything in New York switched off on purpose is a big ask, General we will need to coordinate a conventional attack on the voyagers once the power goes off."

The General nodded in affirmation. In his mind, he thought the president had bottled the best opportunity they had to take out half the remaining voyagers, that this new plan was just a convenient get-out. But he had no choice but to comply and started making calls to coordinate the resources and also brief other military forces on the new plan. Each time he was met with quizzical responses, not entirely convinced this was the way to go.

Once the cabinet had been briefed they set a time when all power would be cut in the greater New York area. At the same time, a bombardment using conventional artillery pieces would commence in an attempt to destroy the group of creatures, still milling around Battery Park.

New Jersey: "Are you serious? We just sit here and watch?" Chad stood next to his chair and was smoking a cigar. He was incredulous.

"Yes, all power will be switched off shortly, the theory is that will prevent them from getting the enormous amount of energy they need to react. They have remained in the same place for some time now and the hypothesis is that they are running low on energy and resting before they move towards the power station. The plan is, we will hit them with heavy artillery and cruise missiles but there's a catch...." The Commanding Officer had assembled the entire unit in a school hall and was briefing the plan.

"Here we go….." Chad said under his breath.

"The catch is, we need to be able to go in on foot and check they are dead once the bombardment is complete. We can't send a drone as there is no way it can tell whether they are deceased, we are going to need you to go in. Now, I've always said I'll be honest with you guys, so in the spirit of that honesty I can tell you that this is not without risk."

There was silence from the Marines as they listened intently. Whilst they didn't sign up to fight alien life forms, they did sign up to serve their country and protect its citizens. This would certainly test their resolve.

"The first objective is to move over to Manhattan, commanders will be briefed separately on the route. You will need to be within a few minutes of their location so I don't need to explain to you what the risk is. When you get into position you will need to kill all power, nothing can be left on, not so much as a cigarette lighter. Understood?"

"Sir" they affirmed in unison.

"We don't know what state they are in and how much power will make a difference once they are attacked so we can't risk anything.

The second point of risk is after the bombardment has commenced. If they are as drained as is thought, they will effectively stay still and die, if not.....if not they are likely to react in a way that has serious consequences. Like I said before, in the spirit of honesty, you'd be unlikely to get out alive."

They remained silent.

"We believe this is what worked in Turkey, there are two pods remaining and the other pod is under observation in the United Kingdom. The government expect this to work there too. We are on the front line in the battle to save humanity from an extinction-level event. Mankind has never faced a challenge like this but, if I was to be asked who I'd want beside me as I face this biblical battle, it's you. I'm not going to take questions, it just remains for me to say that I'm proud to lead you in our country's hour of need......Oorah!!!"

"Oorah" the Marines responded in unison.

Whilst many of them were battle-hardened, never before had they felt their mortality in jeopardy in this way. There was a very real chance they wouldn't survive this and they were relying on a fluke in Turkey, the theories of scientists and the whim of their president. Yet every man and woman in that hall stood up to take on an enemy they didn't understand and that could, in all likelihood, execute them all with no effort.

Manchester, United Kingdom: "Are they taking the piss?! Do they really expect us to believe we can just walk up to these things and it will all be ok, sounds like bloody suicide to me" James had been briefing his soldiers in a car park near the power station, they weren't impressed.

"So who gets the honour of walking towards instant death then sir? I'm taking it you're not stupid enough?" Asked another.

"Look, I understand your concerns" reasoned James.

"You may understand them but there's nothing you can do about it, this is bloody ridiculous" came the response.

"I know how it looks and I agree with some of what you say, but we're soldiers and have a job to do. Now you know I wouldn't ask you to do something I wouldn't do myself, I will be alongside you and I will be the first to approach them if this goes as planned." That seemed to quieten them down somewhat. "The same is going to happen in New York as long as the Voyagers don't move and they are planning to attack first. We don't know if they can communicate with each other over long distances so it's vital we react quickly before they can get a message out. We must assume they are already aware of what happened in Turkey. One last thing from me, once the power goes off, it goes off. No phones, nothing, we cannot afford to take any chances."

"Sir!" they responded, he walked back to his vehicle.

Jet Propulsion Laboratory, California: "He saw it coming you know" Debra was sat talking to Jess, "he saw it coming and even had a theory around how they could find us. The problem is I only had a few words of his theory and he can't remember the rest of it, Power inversion was clearly a part of it but only a tiny part, not enough to jog his memory" she sighed.

"Such a shame, bless him. So you said you'd figured it out, if it wasn't how they got here what was it?" Queried Jess.

"I figured out why and what I guess. The Voyagers are basically interstellar harvesters with an unquenchable thirst for power. They came to earth to harvest it for the power they need to survive. Look at where they have attacked, power stations, homes, businesses. People have been killed but I think that was just a byproduct of them stripping everything they could, I don't think that was their primary objective. Now they've harvested us for so much they're either overfed……and are resting to recharge themselves, or underfed and are recharging before they push on to their next objective. Either way, they've slowed down and now is the time to take them. I think the weak radio signal between Earth and the voyager spacecraft is what guided them here and I believe the success in Turkey was a result of the power cut, power is their site, they can't see without it and were thus incredibly vulnerable."

"And Larry told you all that?"

"No, he just stimulated my brain into thinking it myself. I've told the administrator who said he would tell the president." She took a sip from her coffee, smelling her beverage before doing so. "He awoke my senses, Jess"

"So what happens next?"

"I don't know but what I do know is, nuclear weapons will probably make them stronger and will be disastrous. I hope that rumour is either false or now being reconsidered." In the background, Gus was still prizing apart small pieces of metal with tweezers.

"Well, this is the last of it" Gus declared as he looked at the four pieces of metal he'd pulled apart and was now putting into separate boxes. "I wonder what Larry would have thought if he'd seen what this looks like now.

"Well, I think it would break his heart, so let's be grateful he won't see it close up." Responded Debra. With that, she picked up her purse, threw the last bit of coffee into the sink and wandered out of the door, down the steps and out to her car.

23

Throughout the world, humans had reacted to the attacks by the Voyagers by fleeing population centres and heading to the countryside. Huge refugee camps had sprung up in empty spaces and conditions were barely better than staying put and accepting their fate. Disease was rife and crime and disorder broke out sporadically across these new communities.

Governments were focusing their attention on trying to defeat the voyagers and had allowed these communities to organically grow and where they were Policed, curfews were in place for the majority of the day. In once busy cities, looting was now commonplace and organised crime proliferated rapidly as large parts became 'no go' areas. As power outages increased throughout the world as engineers fled the cities and power stations they once helped maintain, humans revisited the practices of their forefathers. Oil lamps, wood fires and horses were now commonplace. Where possible, humans had moved underground, to subway systems, bunkers, anything else they could find. In New York, a new community was growing up around the underground sewage system, similar communities now existed in other cities across America and the rest of the world.

The British Military were now based in the tunnels under the white cliffs of Dover. Last used during the Second World War and famous for being where the Dunkirk evacuation was planned during World War Two, it was again a bustling epicentre of military activity with miles of tunnels being once again used for the purpose they were dug for back in the Napoleonic conflicts in the 1800s. Elsewhere, Cold War bunkers were reopened and back in use again.

Australians fled towards the outback, Americans to the vast national parks and Africans to the deserts and plains of the continent. Nobody felt safe. Humanity was experiencing the biggest mass movement of people in its existence, society had effectively ceased to exist.

Upper Manhattan, 04:00 hrs. David and Lizzie were getting changed as they'd heard a ferry was going to be sailing over to Jersey City from Battery Park later in the day. The TV was on in the background but flickering on and off as electricity surged and then stopped.

"Are you absolutely sure about this David? It was only yesterday they were trying to shepherd us away from lower Manhattan, how has that changed in twenty-four hours?"

"Well you know I couldn't sleep last night? I waited for you to drop off, got changed and went for a walk. As I was walking across the park (he pointed out of the window) I could see a huddle of cops and listened to them talking. One of them was saying something was going on in lower Manhattan and he'd heard that it was part of a mass evacuation of those left in the City. It makes sense Lizzie doesn't it?" He seemed desperate.

"Well, I guess we've got nothing to lose, what if that's not what's happening though? What will we do?"

"I don't know, I really don't. Hopefully, this early in the morning there will only be a few people around and we can scope it out from a distance."

Lower Manhattan, New York City, 05:00 hrs: The sun was peaking shyly over the top of the giant buildings as this once-teaming city began to wake up. Shafts of light bounced off mirrored windows and birds began to sing a chorus to welcome the new day. The city appeared as it had done every morning for hundreds of years, nothing seemed different, yet it was. A distant buzz could be heard where several military drones had taken to the air to ensure the voyagers remained under close surveillance. They had moved around the park but not strayed more than a few meters from where they had been spotted previously and showed no urgency at all.

'Click' Chad had lost count of how many times he'd checked his magazine was fitted to his M27 Assault rifle correctly, it was a nervous tick he'd had since Helmand in Afghanistan and it was back with a vengeance. He checked his belt for spare mag's and that the holster containing his sidearm was secured. He knew that the reality was that his weapons would probably have little success against the Voyagers, but it made him feel better and took his mind off the silence.

Chads Cougar was parked next to the Vietnam Veterans Memorial on South Street, a road that would normally be heaving with traffic, even at this time in the morning. Today, there was nothing but military vehicles with men and women nervously waiting for the beginning, the attack that could mark the beginning of the end. They mainly stood outside of their vehicles as the warmth of the day began to envelop them, they knew this could be the last time they saw a sunrise and most were keen not to miss it.

"All callsigns this is zero - standby for a broadcast"

Chad felt the butterflies in his stomach and looked across to his crew mate who was just staring straight ahead. He obviously felt Chad's stare, looked back and raised his fist for a well-timed fist pump.

"All callsigns this is zero. Bombardment is due to commence at 06:00 hrs. Power blackout will commence at 05:55 and be marked with a single long tone on the radio. I must remind you that no devices will be permissible from 05:55 and all mobile phones, vehicle engines, radios and even watches must switched off.

Bombardment will commence and once complete, Marines are to go in on foot to ensure they have been dispatched and communicate using hand signals. Again, no radio use until they are confirmed dead. Please be aware you will not have drone coverage at this time.

That is all......good luck"

Chad let out a deep breath. Nearly an hour for them to sit and stew over what was to come, think about what might happen, aware that Voyagers could suddenly move and attack at any time. He found himself thinking about Marie and wondering what she was doing. He hadn't spoken to her for a few days due to there being a ban on electronic devices.

The White House, Washington DC: "Coffee?" The President's secretary was in with a large jug of freshly brewed coffee.

The President had made the decision that he wouldn't leave the traditional seat of the American government despite senior members of the government and military expostulating. He had instructed the vice President to move to the Raven Rock Mountain Complex, also known as Site R, in the mountains of Pennsylvania. This was almost an underground pentagon and he was joined by other senior members of the government and military officials. The president reasoned that, with vast numbers of the US population now on the move out of populated areas, he needed to show leadership and let the public see there was nothing to fear.

"Yes please" responded the President. The President, together with senior military officers and members of his cabinet, were in the 'situation room', deep in the basement of the West Wing. The President had just been briefed on 'Operation Hell's Gate' and was sitting in his comfortable leather chair, talking to his chief of staff. The situation room is far more than a room and is a suite of offices and conference rooms. The main conference room was full of the latest technology so the president could receive full situational awareness, a large dark wooden table and several leather chairs, with the president at the head. "Can I see it happen?" Enquired the president.

"No sir, the power blackout will be happening concurrently so there is no way of getting drones up and the marines will not have any electrical equipment switched on. We should be able to show you the aftermath relatively soon afterwards though, perhaps within ten minutes or so." Responded General Carter.

"Ah I see, no, fair enough"

"I'll get the stream out through to these monitors so we can watch together, you'll find out the same time as me Mr President"

"Thank you General. Will we get footage from the British too?"

"Yes, we have an uplink with the British as they have with us, they should repeat what we are going to do around an hour after us"

Satisfied with the answers, the President took the first sip of his coffee and a bite out of a fresh Danish pastry that had been left on a plate for him by General Carter. The General had warmed slightly to the President over recent days and this was a gesture of goodwill.

Manchester, United Kingdom: James was watching footage of the Voyagers, less than a mile away from where he was parked. They were hardly moving, looking ominous as sunlight glistened off their shiny black and red skin. They were not far from the power station and there was a danger that the Voyagers could get there quickly if they needed to. Because of that, the station had been powered down over the last 24 hours and it was now empty of people and empty of power. The British had decided to start phasing power out some time ago and now the only electronics being used were the CCTV near the voyagers and the tablets being used to monitor them a mile or so away.

The British were incredibly disciplined. Troops positioned closer to the voyagers were using no electronics and were instead using runners between vehicles and semaphores to communicate. The

British Army had gone back in time almost but they were taking absolutely no chances. Vehicles were set up at no more than 200 metres distance from one another and this gave runners shorter distances to travel and made semaphores easier to see between them. On what was now the front line, the Royal Engineers had dug long trenches with underground corridors and tunnels, which went back as far as the rear most vehicles. The tunnels were lit using oil lamps which provided both light and heat. As James watched the Voyagers with interest and wonderment, he heard a tap at the rear of his vehicle.

"Yes"

"Sir" it was a young runner, probably no more than 18 years of age. "You're to turn off the tablets now sir, we are going blind. Any further comm's will be via a runner or semaphore. Start time is at midday precisely, the Americans will be going one hour earlier. We will try to update you after their attack with any lessons learned.

Like their ancestors in the First World War, being a runner was a precarious job, the risks were high and experience low. Whilst colleagues were locked inside armoured vehicles, hidden in trenches or dug-in inside tunnels, the runners were effectively unprotected as they ran across open land from battle line to battle line.

"Thank you" responded James warmly, recognising the young private's tender years. "I'll await further instructions." With that he got back into his vehicle and opened his journal, it was something that was introduced during officer training at the famous Sandhurst Military Academy, James had continued it and used it to reflect. He now felt like he could be writing his very last words.

'Monday, it's ten in the morning and I have been watching our enemy, seemingly oblivious to what we have planned. I don't know if this will work and if it doesn't, I fear these could be my last words. This conflict has brought into focus just how meaningless every conflict man has had between each other was, we were never our biggest threat. Life will never be the same again, even if we are victorious, oh how I would love to go back to living in ignorance

when life was simple. To my parents, thank you for my upbringing,

it shaped me into the man I am today and to my best friend, Chloe,

you will always be in my heart. Finally, to my wife Sarah, you were

my destiny, my companion, my strength, my soul mate and we will

be together always. May god have mercy on our souls.

Major J.Tannick'

Lower Manhattan: "Where is everybody? I mean there's nobody about at all, are you sure about what you heard?" Lizzie was whispering to David as they stood leaning against the railings on Battery Park City Esplanade. They had passed nobody on the way there and could still see no people from where they stood. As they looked out across the calm water, they could see the symbol of their once-great country, the Statue of Liberty. Lady Liberty stood tall despite the threat around her, a shining light for all Americans and a source of strength for both David and Lizzie as they looked across the bay at her.

"Well we're not there yet and it's still really early, can you see any boats?" Responded David. He was focused on a seagull that was bobbing around on the water.

"No, none, maybe it's waiting to go and sitting in dock? What shall we do?"

"I think we'll take a short break and then move on, we need to stay fresh as we don't know what waits for us when we get across the bay" David was concerned. He was expecting to have seen at least Police Officers on their journey across the city but had instead seen nobody, no traffic, no police, nobody at all. They sat on a bench overlooking the water and David pulled a bottle of water from his backpack, taking a well-earned gulp of cold tap water before passing it to Lizzie, whilst wiping his mouth with his sweater.

"Thanks, honey" Lizzie responded.

JPL, California: Gus was still picking through the remains of Voyager One and had managed only five hours of sleep over the last few days. Jess, together with several other scientists were methodically bagging up pieces of the spacecraft and placing them into boxes. It seemed an endless task but they were still focused on their task and the end was in sight.

"Gus, can I ask you something?

"Of course you can Jess" he looked over the top of his spectacles as he responded to her request.

"Can we go outside?" She nodded towards the large glass doors and motioned for them to take their conversation there. Gus was curious. They both stood up and walked towards the doors "coffee?"

"Why not?"

The JPL had long since moved to its backup generator as the electricity supply in the greater Los Angeles area was erratic at best. Earlier in the evening they had taken a large pot out to the car park, lit a fire and boiled some water before pouring it into a giant flask to be used for the evening. They were effectively rationing the electricity they had for key functions.

Jess poured the two drinks into cups and stirred the dark liquid, watching then smelling and almost tasting the aroma of the powdered beverage. She handed one cup to Gus and they both made their way to the doors, Jess grabbed the handle with her free hand and pushed the button down with her thumb before opening it in almost the same motion.

"What's up, Jess?"

"Is this our fault?"

Gus laughed out loud "What? Are you serious?" He suddenly realised she was indeed being serious and the emotion was etched on her face.

"Is there no way we could have destroyed the two spacecraft when we saw the picture and something staring back at us?" She was clutching at straws.

"Oh Jess, no. Firstly there is no way we could have destroyed the two Voyagers, there is no function built into them that would have given us the ability to do that. Perhaps it's something we should have thought of, maybe next time. Secondly, don't forget, by the time we saw that picture those creatures would have likely been well on their way here and almost certainly had realised where we were and that we had something they wanted. Honestly, I think you're overthinking things. Are you ok?" He placed his hand gently on her lower arm to reassure her, she smiled.

"I've heard a rumour. I was listening in to Debra earlier and she's had contact with the scientists working on the bodies from Turkey. Apparently, they dissected one of them to try and understand what they actually are. They ran an electric pulse through it to see how it reacted, bearing in mind this was just a small piece of the animal, and its cells started to regenerate, and the room went ice cold. They had to turn all of the electricity off to stop it from effectively rebuilding itself. What the hell are these creatures from hell Gus, how on earth will we ever stop them?"

"Wow, I hadn't heard that, so even if we do kill them that may not be the end?" He was shocked.

"Doesn't seem like it, no"

"Well, I wonder how long it will be before that gets out. These things are effectively immortal as long as there's an energy supply nearby." He appeared thoughtful as he looked back over the trees and shrubs beyond.

"Well, it will get out sooner or later Gus, it's absolutely terrifying."

"So, thinking about it" Gus was now oblivious to Jess as he thought through what he'd just heard. "Thinking about it, I wonder if they just repair themselves when we attack them, faster than the eye can see. We've been assuming we can't harm them but perhaps that's not the case. Wow Jess, that's huge!" Gus was almost in a trance now, his powerful brain working overtime.

Lower Manhattan, 0545 hrs: "Ok, let's move into battery park then, I'm beginning to get the feeling the rumour I heard last night isn't entirely true" David stood up from the park bench and pulled his backpack over both shoulders. Lizzie stood up a few seconds later and they both made their way along the path adjacent to the waterfront. As they rounded the corner and the park opened up in front of them, David suddenly stopped, straightening his arm across Lizzie's path to ensure she did the same. "What the hell?!"

In front of them were a dozen military drones at various distances, buzzing around the park like bees around their hive. "Well, the city has not been completely abandoned then" quipped David, smiling. Lizzie looked back at him, he held his hand out, she clasped it and he squeezed her hand tight.

In that one moment, as he looked into her beautiful brown eyes, he felt pure love. Love of her, of their life together, of their two beautiful children, of his career, of her passion......

"I don't like this" she mustered a smile back at him. "Wait, do you feel that?!"

"What?" Responded an exasperated David.

"The cold, we've felt this before, it's freezing"

"Yes, yes I can feel it, what the hell........"

And then, nothing.

As David had opened his mouth the cold moved through them at a frightening pace and they were no more. Two children left orphaned and two more victims of the most awesome fighting creatures ever known to man.

The Whitehouse, Washington DC: "Sir, you need to see this." The president followed General Carter into the small briefing room adjacent to the main briefing room, where a screen was set up in front of Colonel Miller who was monitoring both lower Manhattan and Manchester in England, together with a number of their military personnel.

"This has just come in from lower Manhattan sir" he clicked on the screen. It showed a drone shot of battery park and the voyagers on the lawn. In the near distance, David and Lizzie came into the shot, holding hands and they could be seen talking to each other as they inadvertently moved closer to the creatures. Then……they disappeared……and so did the voyagers.

The President moved closer to the screen and looked on in disbelief, "What does this mean?" Queried the president, "And who the hell were those poor people and what in the name of god were they doing there?" He looked around the room for answers. He was quickly disappointed.

"We don't know" responded Col Miller, "we were reassured the area had been cleared of civilian personnel so it's not something we expected."

"Where have they gone?" The president was looking at the screen for the mighty beasts that had just taken two more victims.

"We don't know, troops near the event have reported a sudden blast of extreme cold but as far as we can tell, there are no casualties amongst the military. We will keep looking around the area for them and react as soon as we see them. We will keep you updated Mr President."

The president had one arm folded across his face and held his hand over his mouth as his eyes welled up.

"God damn it!" The president suddenly thumped the table and walked back out to the main room. The Colonel took a deep breath and blew his fringe.

Manchester, United Kingdom 1005 hrs: tap, tap. "Sir" a runner was again at Major Tanick's vehicle. "Sir, there's been a development"

It was five minutes after the attack was due to commence in New York, James assumed it was an update but the look on the runner's face suggested otherwise.

"Go on"

"It's the Americans sir, they've lost them"

"What do you mean lost them private?" The confusion on his face was easy to read.

"Well sir, two civilian personnel strayed into battery park and then disappeared along with the voyagers, the hypothesis is they have been killed and the Voyagers have moved off."

"What do you mean 'moved off'?"

"They can no longer be seen sir, they've vanished" This was the third commander he'd had this exact conversation with as he went between command vehicles.

"Are we still proceeding as planned?"

"Yes sir, mid day, watch for the flags then move on foot once the bombardment finishes."

"Thank you, now take care of yourself private" he smiled, he knew how precarious his task was.

"I will sir, thank you"

Major Tannick closed the vehicle's door and rubbed his eyes. He suddenly pulled his left hand away from his eyes and noticed his hands were shaking uncontrollably like he was cold, 'adrenaline' he thought to himself before rubbing his hands together. The Americans were no longer going to prove the concept, lessening the risk to the British. They would now be going first and he knew what a risk that was. In the back of his mind he had known that, if the Americans had been destroyed, their attack would likely have been called off whilst there was a rethink of tactics.

The Whitehouse, Washington DC: "Should we move the artillery sir, seems pointless keeping them in the one place we now know the Voyagers aren't don't you think?" General Carter was on the phone to the ground deployed commander in New York, General Peters. General Peters was an incredibly experienced military strategist and very keen to keep the pressure on.

"No, it's too soon and where are we going to move them? Let's hope they return somewhere near their last location and we can continue as we had previously planned. Hold your nerve, General."

"Yes, sir" responded General Peters.

Manchester 11:55 hrs: Major Tannick looked down at his analogue watch, hand still shaking. He glanced at his rifle, glistening with gun oil, moved the dust cover on the side of the weapon and could see a gold, shiny round of ammunition sitting proudly, ready to be fired. He was standing next to his vehicle as he'd given up on trying to sit still some time ago. Time had actually passed relatively quickly up until this point but now his focus had gone up a level and time ticked by slowly. Within his field of vision were dozens of military vehicles and personnel, all looking towards where the voyagers were last spotted. To the left of his view was the churned earth left by another vehicle and he watched a tiny robin redbreast hopping around, pulling its tasty lunch from the earth. As James looked at the small bird, he wondered if this would be his last memory. He looked up to see white flags being raised across the battlefront. This was it, this was the end.......

Manhattan: "Seriously, I cannot believe it man!" News had just reached Chad and the other Marines that their plans would have to change. "So they have no idea where they are, what were they thinking getting in the way?"

"Well I don't think they're thinking anything now Chad, I think that was a very Salutary lesson learned, god bless them."

"Sure, damn it, you're right. We are still here I suppose. What next I wonder? The radio has been quiet for a while, I guess they're trying to figure out what next. Did you feel that chill earlier, it must have been them"

"Yeh, not good"

Manchester:

WOOSH, WOOSH, WOOSH, WOOSH!!

BOOM!!

Rockets and artillery flew over the heads of James and his team, pummeling the target area. It was a magnificent site as massive guns unleashed their giant shells and M270's launched rocket, after rocket, after rocket. In front of the battlefield, all that could be seen was fire. 'This must be what hell looks like' thought James as he and his troops started to jog towards their starting point. Waiting, wondering.......

After fifteen minutes of rockets and shells, silence fell again and then.......

Pheep........whistles, similar to those used in the First World War to direct men to go over the top, were blown to signify the next phase. James and his troops were in a line beyond the last trench. He ran forward, rifle drawn, bayonet fixed, leading his troops towards the threat. The area was covered in a thick cloud of smoke from the ordinance, as he burst through he was suddenly greeted by a blast of ice-cold air, and then

Nothing........

The Whitehouse, Washington DC: "They're back!!" Shouted Colonel Miller from the adjacent room. "Sir, they're back" the president ran towards the officer with General Carter just behind him.

"What? What do you mean?" Asked the president urgently.

"They're back sir, look."

The president and all those with him stared at the screen to see the Voyagers, back in Battery Park (if they ever left) pretty much as they were before.

"And sir, the British have commenced their attack, we are waiting to hear from them" updated the intelligence officer.

"Thank you, Colonel. General, are we going to commence our attack?!"

"But sir, shouldn't we wait to hear how the British got on first?"

"General, the future of mankind depends on what we do next, I for one don't want to lose site of them again, do you? No General, we attack them and we do it now. Get that god damn electricity off and kill those god damn sons of bitches!!" A mild mannered man, this was the first time most of them had witnessed him lose his temper.

Manhattan: Chad was watching as he saw a Marine running from vehicle to vehicle, he eventually made it to Chad and his crew mates.

"The attack will commence in five minutes, you are to move up towards the outskirts of the park, next to the ferry terminal, and await a whistle blast to commence the second phase." The British had shared their approach and the Americans were now adapting it as their own. "Power will be cut immediately before the bombardment commences, do you understand?"

"I do, yes." Chad got out of his vehicle and put his rifle across his chest, tightening his sling so they almost became one. He started to walk towards the ferry terminal together with his fellow Marines.

As he did so, the power supply to the city was being cut off, block by block, until

PHT!!

All power was out, then.....

WOOSH, WOOSH, WOOSH, WOOSH!!

BANG!!

Missiles, rockets and artillery pieces smashed into Battery Park. Chad could feel the air pressure changes as a cruise missile flew past his head. This was shock and awe on another scale. Fifteen minutes of hell raining down on Battery park was followed by silence and then......

PHEEP!

Dozens of whistles marked the final phase and Chad started to run forwards with his fellow Marines. Years of combat training had come to this, the final battle, he was almost sprinting through the clouds of smoke that had suddenly filled the park from the numerous explosions. As he ran he could hear shouts as Marines let out their war cry as they neared the target, more through fear than anything else. Suddenly, he could see shards of light breaking through the grey clouds of smoke, then it began to clear completely. Suddenly he was hit by a wall of ice cold air and then

Nothing.........

The Whitehouse: "Well?" Asked the President.

"Well, we just wait sir, this is the worst part" replied General Carter.

Ring, ring........the presidents PA picked up his phone.

"Sir, it's for you, it's the British Prime Minister......."

Manchester: James heart was in his mouth as he broke through the smoke and was shocked by what confronted him. Soldiers, several rows deep, stood together staring, staring at a mass of black and red creatures strewn across the ground. It was the first time he'd seen one. He pushed past his soldiers and held his rifle up, ensured the bayonet was fixed, and thrust it into the body of one of the creatures. It didn't move. He thrust it into a second.....nothing. It was cold, nothing was moving. He looked around and felt like he wanted to cheer, but didn't.

Manhattan: As the smoke cleared completely, Chad could see one of the creatures body thrown across one of the park benches. He ran up to it with his rifle drawn and thrust his bayonet into its body. No reaction.

PHEEP, PHEEP!!

Two whistle blasts marked success and before he could talk to anybody, there was an overwhelming force of drones in the air, surveying the battlefield, ready to report the success to the country's leaders.

The Whitehouse, Washington DC: The President sat back in his large leather chair, phone in hand. Everybody in the room was staring at him, they could hear a pin drop. All of a sudden he looked up, mouthing 'thank you god' as he did so. The screen in front of them suddenly sprung to life and there were two live links, one showing Chad and his fellow Marines in Battery Park, standing beside the carcasses of dead voyagers, the second showed Major James Tannick and his troops, stood likewise in Manchester. The rooms erupted into cheers as the news got out that all voyagers had now been accounted for.

24

The Whitehouse, Washington DC: "Three, two, one, we're live sir"

"My fellow Americans. It is with relief that I can tell you and the people of the world, that the voyagers have been defeated. Together, mankind has stood together to defeat the greatest threat known to man, we have succeeded. We must now take time to grieve for our dead, then we must come back stronger than we've ever been, together. It won't be easy and it will take time but you can start tonight, by returning to your homes. I have spoken to my fellow world leaders and our priority is now to restore law and order, so rest assured you will feel safe once again. But whilst we want to restore normality, things will never be the same again. We must ensure there is no repeat and to do that we must work together, and this will be my focus in the months and years to come. God bless our dead and god bless the United States of America."

The president was sat behind his desk in the Oval Office and looked relaxed. It was the first time in days he had been smartly dressed in his jacket and tie and he finally felt human again. The First Lady walked up to him as the cameras switched off and kissed him gently on the forehead.

"What now?" The First Lady asked.

"Vacation?" The president responded playfully. He was joking if course, so much work would now be needed, the President's work was just beginning. They walked out of his office and back to their living quarters where the President went to bed to recharge.

JPL, California: The team were watching the Presidents broadcast on the large screens and cheers broke out across the room. Debra was sat on a stool in the corner of the room smiling gently and thinking about her great friends Larry and Barbara, wondering if they were even watching. Jess was sat next to Gus, she tapped him on the shoulder, he looked around.

"There's still something" Jess still looked concerned.

"Oh come on Jess, what do you mean, this is a great day?" Responded Gus, smiling to reassure her.

"I don't know I just feel uneasy, I don't know, I just feel like this isn't all over."

"Look, mankind has been on this planet a long time and that was the first time we've been visited......"

"That we know of" interrupted Jess.

"Yes, that we know of, I agree. But the chances of it happening again any time soon are slim even if we take no steps to prevent it, let alone if we do."

"I just, I can't explain it, I'm sorry" Jess responded.

"Don't be sorry, just enjoy the moment, we will never feel like this again in our lifetime." With that, they both stood up and Gus gave Jess a long hug and kissed her cheek, she smiled.

Several days later, the Whitehouse, Washington DC: The President was at his desk. He had worked relentlessly the previous few days as the rebuild began. "So, these things can regenerate themselves?"

"Yes Mr President, their cells seem to regenerate whenever they are near an energy source, that's obviously what they were feeding on. So we have all the body's, they won't set on fire, we've tried that, they don't melt. We have looked at the safest and most effective way to dispose of them and we have two options. One, we launch them into space, the problem with that is there are so many energy sources in space they could regenerate and come back. Secondly, we dissect them into small pieces and bury them. That's our preferred option." Responded General Carter. He was stood with the NASA Administrator and both men looked deeply concerned. It was an issue that had occupied both men and their teams for most of the previous days.

"Really? That doesn't sound very safe to me. Can you imagine people digging them up." The President looked puzzled.

"No sir, nobody will be digging them up where we are going to bury them"

Eleven Kilometres above the Mariana Trench, the Pacific Ocean, rain crashing down: "What the hell is in these things?" Hans Van Kleeft was carefully guiding his cargo ship above the deepest part of the ocean. Eleven Kilometers below them lay the bottom of the world, a deep, dark place where light rarely reaches.

"No idea sir, and if I did I couldn't tell you, it's classified." Responded the US Navy Commander who had joined the ship from Guam, together with several large, heavy, lead-lined titanium cases.

"I've never known so much activity in this area, there's been a number of ships with subs going down there for a few days now. Makes you wonder doesn't it?" Replied Van Kleeft. The Naval man just stared at him. Van Kleeft realised there was no point in asking any more questions so he stepped outside of the bridge and walked down to the main deck. The sun was shining and the wind was low as he walked towards the huge cases. Several other ships were in the vicinity and it was clear these cases weren't just being dropped into the ocean as he could see several subs were preparing to go down with them.

"Ok, we are directly over the target area, you said these things have a motor and will guide them where they need to go. This is the best start you can have." Van Kleeft nodded at his crane operator. He took the joystick in his right hand and started to manoeuvre the first container over the side of the ship. The Commander looked visibly concerned as he felt the ship list to one side as it hovered over the open water, then the crane operator pressed a button with his free hand and it splashed down into the water.

Two hundred meters away, a bright yellow sub disappeared under the surface.

Beep……..beep.

"I'm under and heading down, do you have the control?" The sub-operator pointed his machine down towards the ocean floor and followed the container down for four hours until it hit the bottom. On the Ocean bed were several holes that had been dug in the previous days using subs. The operator managed to guide the container into one of the graves and the sub-operator used some sub attachments to ensure they were covered. One by one, over a period of days and a number of return journeys from Guam, they were all buried in the deepest part of the ocean.

White House, Washington DC: "That's it sir, they're all gone, all buried." The president's Chief of Staff had brought the morning papers into the president to chat through some of the headlines and their progress towards restoring normality. "I finally feel like that's it, it's over."

"I hope so old friend, I really do" responded the President as he walked towards the two sofas, picked up his cup of coffee from the table, and then sat back down. " I just have this horrible feeling, you know, that I can't shake."

"That's understandable, none of us have ever been through something like this before, it looked like it was the end for a while I really thought we were gonners," he smiled as he placed his hand on the wrist of the president, who was now sat on the opposite sofa.

"You know? You're probably right" he smiled back, picked up the Wall Street journal and started looking at the sections that had been highlighted for him.

25

In the years that followed, humans carried on exploring space but did so with more knowledge of what was out there and so a great deal more caution. All nations were joined in lessening mankind's footprint in space, masking the electrical noises coming from our planet, ensuring our radios signals outside of our atmosphere were disguised and stopping any attempts to contact other beings.

President Williams was seen in a new light. Previously perceived to be a poor decision-maker and weak leader, he was now seen as strong and decisive and enjoyed an unprecedented lead in the polls and near complete popularity across the Country regardless of political persuasion.

Sherri went on to work with charities to rebuild communities and help the vulnerable restore their lives. Her influence during the worlds darkest hours was not understated if, for no other reason, than the fact her husband spoke glowingly about the strength she had given him. The First Lady was as popular as the President and they made a formidable team.

As humans counted the human cost of the Voyagers invasion, one thing became abundantly clear. Man's greatest enemy is not each other. The human race was left able to prosper once more not because they fought each other, didn't look after the vulnerable and allowed inequality to pervade, it prospered because humans pulled together and worked as one. It became clear that what binds people is far greater than what makes us different. War on earth ended and greater efforts were made to end hunger and deprivation across the planet. A single space force, a coalition of every nation on earth and run in a similar way to NATO, was established.

Finally, and most importantly, humans had answered the question as to whether life existed outside our planet and it had become clear we should listen more effectively to people like Professor Stephen Hawking who, as humans sent more and more messages out to space, warned that any civilisation that could actually read a message, would likely need to be billions of years ahead of us in development.

"If so they will be vastly more powerful and may not see us as any more valuable than we see bacteria."

Wise words.......

As the end became more obvious, Debra looked back at her life with a little regret. Rather than dwell on this however, she decided to retire almost immediately and go home, back to Maine. She moved back into her parents old house and spent her time around the lake, fishing, boating and meeting people. She also joined the local amateur astronomy club where she went back to her childhood hobby of staring through a telescope at the wonderment of the stars. It was there that she met Gerry, with whom she established a great friendship and a companion for her later years.

Jess quickly became one of the most important members of the JPL team, gaining her Doctorate soon after. Gus was to get his wish too, moving onto the Mars programs before becoming project lead, he didn't intend to stop there and ambitiously had the NASA administrator post in his sites.

Larry and Barbara continued to spend their days walking little Charlie through the forest largely oblivious to the wider world and the impact of the alien invasion. More regularly in touch with Debra than before the Voyagers attack, they frequently met up with her and Gerry in Maine, eating at their favourite restaurant together and walking around the lake.

Ethan and Emily Harris grew up with their grandparents. David's passion for space and science had rubbed off on both of them and they were both keen astronomers. They'd often store through a telescope, imagining they could see their parents in the stars, it helped them heal.

Chad returned home and left the Marines soon after. Marie couldn't cope with the deployments and wanted to spend more time with him so he put his unique view of the war to good use and started a successful YouTube channel based on what he had seen.

James Tannick returned home to Sarah and was soon promoted to the rank of Lieutenant Colonel in recognition of his outstanding leadership during the conflict. It wasn't enough to keep him in the British Army, however, and he retired soon after. Once retired, James published his journal of the war to critical acclaim, leading to a successful writing career. They settled in North Yorkshire and James and Sarah spent their days walking their dogs in the almost permanent drizzle as James new career exploded.

Several years later:

"How much longer are they gonna be down there?" The US Navy Officer asked for a third time as he lit his cigar on the deck of the large white ship bobbing gently on top of the Ocean. The boat captain was beginning to lose his patience as he clasped his radio in one hand whilst steadying himself with the other by holding onto the side rail. Several miles below a small yellow submarine was at the bottom of the Mariana Trench.

"Yes I'm nearly there. Readings are all normal, all levels look good" David Sanchez was on a routine monitoring mission to check all was well with the titanium cases. "Still can't see a great deal."

"Yes it's been choppy for the last few days, probably won't clear up until you're closer to the bottom" responded the boat captain.

"Well I'm only three hundred meters away.........two hundred, that's strange, the temperature has just dropped suddenly".......then

Nothing.

The end.

www.mileskentbooks.co.uk

Printed in Great Britain
by Amazon

37684541R00235